S0-BNW-412

78

THE
SPIRIT CALLER

JEAN HAGER

THE MYSTERIOUS PRESS

Published by Warner Books

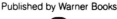

A Time Warner Company

Mysterious Press books are published by Warner Books, Inc.,
1271 Avenue of the Americas, New York, NY 10020.

 A Time Warner Company

The Mysterious Press name and logo are registered trademarks of Warner Books, Inc.

Printed in the United States of America

First printing: May 1997

10   9   8   7   6   5   4   3   2   1

Library of Congress Cataloging-in-Publication Data
Hager, Jean.
    The spirit caller / Jean Hager.
        p.   cm.
    ISBN 0-89296-640-8
    I. Bearpaw, Molly (Fictitious character)—Fiction.   2. Women
detectives—Oklahoma—Fiction.   3. Cherokee Indians—Fiction.
4. Oklahoma—Fiction.   I. Title.
PS3558.A3232S65   1997
813'.54—dc20   96-42033
                                                                       CIP

THE
SPIRIT CALLER

MYSTERY NOVELS BY JEAN HAGER

Featuring Molly Bearpaw

THE SPIRIT CALLER
SEVEN BLACK STONES
THE REDBIRD'S CRY
RAVENMOCKER

Featuring Chief Mitchell Bushyhead

THE FIRE CARRIER
GHOSTLAND
NIGHT WALKER
THE GRANDFATHER MEDICINE

Dedicated to Genell Dellin, Teresa Miller, Marilyn Pappano, and Renee Wilson with love and gratitude for their friendship and support.

Acknowledgments

The author wishes to express special thanks to the following people for their help in research. Any errors remaining are mine, not theirs.

Phil Quaile, Paintmaster, Tulsa, OK; Kathy Smithson, Cherokee County Sheriff's Department, Tahlequah, OK; Pat Ragsdale, Cherokee Nation Marshal Service, Tahlequah, OK; Sequoyah Guess, Sandy Long, and Marsha Soap, Tsa-La-Gi Library, Tahlequah, OK; and Ralph D. Copeland, Crane, TX.

Author's Note

Although some streets and locations referred to in this novel are authentic, others are figments of the author's imagination—the Native American Research Library, Dowell's Foreign Cars, and the Indian Baptist Church on Willis Road are fictitious, as are all the characters, incidents, and dialogue. Any resemblance to actual events, places, or persons, living or dead, is entirely coincidental.

THE
SPIRIT CALLER

Listen! Ha! You have strayed from the pathway. Now you have drawn near to hearken. You are resting directly overhead.

1

Molly paused outside her office door to admire the black-bordered gilt letters on the glass pane.

Major Crimes Unit
Cherokee Nation of Oklahoma
Molly Bearpaw, Investigator

After four months in her new job, reading the words still gave her a thrill, even if the entire unit was contained in this one small office.

She thrust her key into the keyhole, but it resisted her efforts to twist it to the left. The door was already unlocked. She opened it and stuck her head in.

"Good mornin', Molly." Natalie Wind's voice twanged with the languid vowels of rural southeastern Oklahoma. Clad in jeans and a T-shirt, Nat stood behind the institutional-gray metal desk which faced the door, pouring hot water from a small electric pot into a mug. She kept the pot, a box of tea bags, and two mugs, decorated with the Cherokee Nation seal, on a small tray on the desk. A white paper sack sat next to the tray.

Molly stepped in and closed the door. She tossed her purse at her desk. It hit the corner and fell to the floor.

"Nice shot." Natalie deposited the pot on the tray and plucked a tea bag from the box.

"Isn't this Friday?"

"It sure was the last time I looked."

"So what are you doing here?" Natalie usually worked on Monday, Tuesday, Wednesday, and Thursday afternoons.

"The prof dismissed my eight o'clock bio lab." Natalie swished the tea bag around, then leaned over her desk and dropped it in the wastebasket. "I don't have anything else until one, so I thought I'd catch up on some paperwork." She picked up the mug in both hands. "God knows I can use the money."

The tribal council had approved up to twenty-five hours a week for Molly's assistant but, to Natalie's chagrin, she was rarely able to find that much free time from classes and studying. It wasn't only that she needed the money, either. She was a prelaw student at Northeastern State University in Tahlequah and aspired to be a prosecutor when she finished law school. Despite the fact that she did the work of a clerk-typist, she persisted in viewing her job as an apprenticeship in criminal investigation.

Molly retrieved her purse. "Shouldn't you be hitting the books?" The spring semester would end in two weeks, which left only one week before final exams.

Natalie sipped her tea, reacting to Molly's question with a careless shrug. "Plenty of time. I'm a crammer." She tipped her head toward the white paper sack on her desk. "I got a couple of Danish at Morgan's. Want one?" Homemade pastries from Morgan's Bakery, next door to The Shack café on the main street, were light as air and melted like spun sugar in the mouth.

"I already had breakfast," Molly said, her gaze lingering on the cheese Danish that Natalie pulled from the sack.

Natalie gave her an amused smile and bit into the pastry, dislodging tiny sugar crystals which drifted to the floor.

"Oh, what the heck." Molly stuffed her purse in a desk drawer, then made herself a cup of tea and took it and the remaining Danish back to her desk. The same desk in the same office she'd occupied as a Native American Advocacy League investigator. With the addition of Natalie's desk, there was barely room left for four chairs—including the desk chairs—and two file cabinets.

But Molly would never complain about the cramped quarters. She felt lucky to have the job. The federal grant that had funded her salary had run out last year, and for a while it had looked as though she would have to leave Tahlequah to find work. About the time she'd begun to line up interviews, the tribal council had come up with the money for her salary and created a new position for her.

Briefly the major crimes unit had been a part of the tribal police-security force. But the new Cherokee Nation Marshal Service had recently replaced the force. Now fourteen marshals, eleven officers, and three investigators helped patrol ten counties of the Nation's original fourteen-county area. Since the reorganization, Molly reported directly to the council.

The only outward changes in her status were the lettering on the door, the 9-millimeter semiautomatic Smith & Wesson she'd been issued, and Natalie, her part-time assistant. Natalie and the new title were welcome changes. As for the gun, after she'd passed the gun safety course required for a license to carry, the Smith & Wesson had remained locked in the glove compartment of her car. She *had* made one concession to the potential dangers of her new job, though—a small cylinder of pepper spray attached to her key ring.

Natalie finished her Danish, licked her fingers and wiped them on a paper napkin. Eyeing Molly's red cotton shirt and full, flowered skirt, she asked, "Is D.J. picking you up for lunch or something?" Natalie liked Sheriff Deputy D.J. Kennedy, with whom Molly had had a relationship for over a year, and had once described him as "seriously cute."

"Nope." Molly tugged open the window beside her desk, pushing it up as far as it would go. Gathering her long skirt around her legs, she settled into her chair. "D.J.'s working the night shift this month. Besides, since when do I dress up for D.J.?" Molly didn't dress up, period, except on rare occasions to please her grandmother, who bought her feminine dresses for birthdays and Christmas.

"I haven't done my laundry yet this week," Molly added. "All my jeans are dirty."

"Sometimes I think you take D.J. for granted."

"Because I prefer jeans to dresses? That's some leap in logic."

"It's not that, it's just—"

"Go ahead, say it."

"Sometimes I get the feeling you keep him at arm's length—oh, well, it's none of my business."

No, it wasn't, but Molly understood what Natalie meant. But Natalie didn't understand what Molly had been through. Once she'd let a man become her reason for living and, when it was over, she'd had to rebuild her life from the ground up. She was terrified of making that mistake again. Consequently, she had a near-phobic fear of commitment. But she was working on it.

Nat had opened a file folder and was leafing through it.

Molly put aside thoughts of D.J. and spent a few moments making a mental to-do list for the day. She had several follow-up phone calls to make, tying up loose ends on a couple of cases, and some letters to write, requesting documents and information on other cases. It was a slow time, between winding up several jobs and taking on new ones. Even the weather enticed her to take it easy. A day like this one wasn't made for work.

Molly leaned back in her chair, facing the window. The morning sun lit the pure blue sky behind the Muskogee Avenue storefronts. A light breeze scattered a few lacy clouds and wafted through the window, bringing the scent of pine from the Kiamichi mountain country to the south to mingle with the sweet smells of Anasku'tee, the planting moon.

Alternately nibbling the pastry and sipping tea, Molly inhaled the fragrance of spring in Cherokee County. Her gaze drifted up Muskogee Avenue, taking in several blocks of Tahlequah's main street, which bordered Cherokee Square on the west. Redbuds and dogwoods bloomed profusely, decorating the town with opulent pink and white blossoms. Along the sidewalk, petunias and marigolds spilled from wooden tubs.

She loved spring in Tahlequah when it was at its most

beautiful. For years, the attractions of the little university town tucked in among Ozark foothills had been known by few. But that was changing. Recently a national magazine had named Tahlequah one of the best one hundred small towns in America, noting that its population was increasing by three percent annually. Nobody seemed to know who the new people were, since no new industries had come to town. Probably most of the additional residents were retirees, moving closer to recreational areas at Grand Lake and the Illinois River. Molly had mixed feelings about the publicity and worried that it might make the town grow too big. She liked Tahlequah just the way it was.

"Oh. I almost forgot." Natalie waved a pink phone message slip. "Your grandmother called. She said it's important."

"What's important?"

"Something about Sunday."

"Sunday?" Molly searched her memory and finally recalled a conversation she'd had with Eva a couple of weeks ago. "The wild onions must be ready." Hard to believe it was May already.

"Say what?"

"The Indian Baptist Church has a wild onion breakfast every year about this time. Actually, it's more a potluck lunch with scrambled eggs and wild onions as the featured dish."

"Hey, my aunt goes to that church."

"Talia Wind?"

Natalie nodded. Her aunt Talia was a self-professed conjurer who lived at Eagle Rock, a quasi-religious compound outside of Tahlequah. The small community of three or four dozen people had come into being when a Cherokee medicine man named Agasuyed parceled his farm into small acreages which he sold to some of his followers. Agasuyed—"chosen" in Cherokee—claimed to have received the name as well as powerful medicine in a series of visions from the spirit of an ancient Cherokee priest. Molly had heard that he'd even gone to court to make the name legal.

The goal of the community was said to be a return to the old Indian reverence for animals, the earth, and the forces of nature. From what Molly had heard, a few of them, including Talia Wind, flavored ancient Indian wisdom with generous sprinklings of New Age ideas.

About a year ago, Talia Wind had moved into the compound with her husband, Dell Greer, who had reportedly become Agasuyed's right-hand man. Then rumors circulated that a power struggle was going on between Talia Wind and Agasuyed for spiritual leadership of the community. Next thing anyone knew, Talia and Greer were divorced; but Talia had stayed with the group, having received some land and a mobile home in the divorce settlement.

"I love scrambled eggs and wild onions," Natalie was saying. "If Aunt Talia's going to that breakfast, I may invite myself to go along."

"How are things out at Eagle Rock?" Molly asked.

"Okay, I guess. It's been a couple of weeks since I talked to Talia. My brother, Ridge, told me that Dell and that disgusting slob Agasuyed are trying to force her out, but she's still there."

"Frankly, I'm surprised to hear that Talia attends a traditional church," Molly said.

"It's true she's into talking to animal spirits and reading medicine cards and stuff like that," Nat interpreted.

"Not exactly Southern Baptist orthodoxy." On the other

hand, neither was using the services of a medicine man, which Molly's grandmother had been known to do.

"Aunt Talia *has* had some heated discussions with the minister. He doesn't approve of her."

Molly swallowed the last of her tea. "Why does that not surprise me?"

Natalie gave an airy wave of her hand. "Aunt Talia says there's room in the world for all religions and beliefs. She thought that's what Eagle Rock was all about when she and Dell moved out there. She organized meditation groups and vision quests for the women." Agitated now, Nat raked her fingers through her bangs. She was one-quarter Cherokee, but didn't look it in spite of dark eyes and straight, black hair worn in a short, shiny cap. Natalie got her fair complexion from her Swedish mother. The contrast of brownish black eyes looking at you from Natalie's pale, oval face was often startling. Especially when those eyes were wide, as now, and flashing with indignation. "It really shocked Talia when Agasuyed started saying she was a big fraud and an evil, forward woman."

Molly fingered the pewter turtle paperweight on her desk. In Cherokee folk tales, Turtle was a great trickster. You never quite knew what was going on in Turtle's mind. *Like you,* D.J. had said when he presented her with the paperweight.

She looked up at Nat. "You make Agasuyed sound like a chauvinist."

Natalie's head bobbed. "Classic case. Basically, he wanted Aunt Talia to sit down and shut up. Can you believe that garbage? Cherokee women have always been equal with men. Why, Wilma Mankiller was the first female chief of a major Indian tribe. There were even women warriors in the old days, like the Beloved Woman—can't think of her English name . . ."

"Nancy Ward."

"That's it. Somebody should remind Agasuyed of Nancy Ward when he gets on his soapbox about going back to the old ways."

"Maybe Talia has."

"Yeah, for all the good it would do."

"How are the other people at Eagle Rock reacting to this—um, disagreement between Agasuyed and your aunt?"

Natalie pursed her lips. "At first they ignored it, but Agasuyed wouldn't let it go. So they've been forced to take sides. Aunt Talia has a dozen or so followers, all women, and the others stuck with Agasuyed."

"Including Dell Greer, I take it."

"Yeah," she said, frowning. "It really hurt Aunt Talia that her own husband expected her to buckle under to Agasuyed."

"Can't say I blame her." Turf battle. How predictable. It happened in every group in the world, even groups of only two or three people.

"They weren't getting along too well to start with," Natalie went on, "but when Dell took sides with Agasuyed, that was the last straw and she divorced him. Between you and me, I think she's got a new boyfriend. She's real secretive about it, though."

"I'm surprised she stayed at Eagle Rock."

"Join the club. Everybody out there expected her to leave. I think she still gets the cold shoulder from some of those people."

"Maybe she stayed because the new boyfriend is there."

Natalie gave the idea some consideration. "You know, I hadn't thought of that. Could be."

"Well, the opposition to Talia will eventually die down," Molly said. "They're all living so close together, they have to deal with each other. It's hard to hold grudges under those conditions."

"I hope you're right," Natalie said, but disbelief edged her voice.

"Nat, are you worried about your aunt?"

"I guess I am." Natalie used both hands to tuck the ends of her hair behind her ears. "Oh, it's probably nothing."

"What is?"

"Aunt Talia has received some anonymous hate mail."

"Do you mean threatening mail?"

Natalie hesitated. "Sort of. The notes tell her to get out of Eagle Rock if she knows what's good for her."

"Then maybe she should leave."

Natalie shook her head. "That would be deserting her followers. Besides, it's the principle of the thing. Aunt Talia is more determined than ever to stay." She gnawed anxiously on the cap of a ballpoint pen. "The last time I saw Aunt Talia, she had some ugly bruises on one arm. She *said* she got them when she fell down the steps of her mobile home."

"You don't believe that's what happened?"

"I'm not sure, but she changed the subject real quick."

"You think Dell Greer did it?"

Natalie took the pen from her mouth and tossed it on the desk. "It wouldn't surprise me. Him or another one of Aga-suyed's followers, trying to scare her into leaving."

"Did she report it to the police?"

"No, and I don't know why." Natalie held Molly's gaze

for a long moment. "Maybe she really did fall down the steps." She wheeled her chair around to face their new-used computer—the council had finally heeded Molly's request and found one somewhere.

Molly let the topic of Talia Wind go, stifling her misgivings. She didn't really know Talia, but assumed she knew what she was doing.

Remembering her grandmother's message, Molly reached for the phone and dialed Eva's number in Park Hill.

"Are you coming to the wild onion breakfast Sunday?" Eva asked when they'd exchanged greetings.

"As far as I know," Molly said. "What time is it again?"

"Eleven."

Through the open window, Molly watched a couple walking their poodle across Cherokee Square. At the northeast corner of the square, they turned in the direction of Town Branch Park, prompting Molly to consider getting take-out for lunch and eating in the park.

"What should I bring?" she asked Eva.

"Not a thing. I'll take enough for both of us."

"Okay." Molly was more than willing to agree; she wasn't a great cook, unlike Eva and the other women who attended the Indian Baptist Church. Molly knew this because she'd been to their potlucks before. If Sunday's weather was like today's, they'd eat outside, under the wide-spreading branches of old oaks and elms.

"You promise you'll be there, then?" Eva's tone was tense.

The bucolic picture of bright sun, deep shade, and country spaces that Molly's imagination had been painting faded away. Belatedly, Eva had her full attention. "Why is this so important to you?" Eva frequently invited Molly to attend church services with her, but never with so much persistence.

"I didn't say it was important."

"I can tell when you've got something weighing on your mind. What's wrong, Grandmother?"

"Nothing," Eva said sharply and too quickly. She might as well have been saying everything was fine while watching rising floodwaters surround her house. But you couldn't press Eva to reveal what was on her mind until she was ready.

"I just want to see you," Eva said finally.

"I want to see you, too," Molly told her. No use pointing out that she made frequent trips to visit Eva in Park Hill, that she had, in fact, seen Eva earlier in the week.

Before Molly could ask another question, Eva hung up.

Nothing's wrong. Which might not be literal truth, Molly mused, but it must mean there was nothing to worry about.

Then why did she feel so uneasy?

O Black Raven, you never fail in anything.

2

At the house of Agasuyed Beaver in the Eagle Rock community, Dell Greer stood on the porch and listened to the fat man rant.

"Damn evil woman," he said in his wheezy voice. *"Suna'yi eda'hi!"*

"A night goer?" Dell, though three-eighths Cherokee, did not speak the language and could only understand a word now and then. Agasuyed knew that. Sometimes Dell thought he spoke Cherokee just to irritate him. "A witch?"

Agasuyed thrust himself forward in his chair. His double chins wobbled. *"Do'-yu,* yes! That wife of yours is a witch! You must stop those ceremonies. She leads the women astray."

Stop Talia doing something she had her head set on doing? Oooh, yeah. Might as well try to hold back an avalanche with your hands. "She's not my wife," Dell said in a resigned voice. He leaned his bony hip against the porch post and raked stringy black hair out of his eyes. Fishing a toothpick out of his T-shirt pocket, he began picking his teeth. "I have no control over what she does." Talia had a stubborn streak a mile wide. He hadn't realized it until after they were married, though he should have suspected when she refused to take his name, even when he begged her. It still rankled that he hadn't seen Talia's true nature, but he'd been in the grip of testosterone at the time. Hormones are blind.

Agasuyed wore his long hair tied back with what looked like a discarded shoestring. Because of his obesity, his wardrobe consisted almost entirely of coveralls or overalls, ordered from the Sears big man's catalogue, with T-shirts or flannel shirts, depending on the weather. At the moment, he wore overalls with no shirt at all.

"She causes contention among my people!" Agasuyed wheezed. "She will destroy Eagle Rock!" He held his bulging body stiff in his chair, his face rigid with contempt.

Agasuyed liked to refer to the people at Eagle Rock as *his* people, but from what Greer had seen of Cherokees, most of them were like Talia, about as herdable as hogs on ice.

Greer thought he heard movement behind the house. It was probably Agasuyed's wife, Ina, tending her vegetable garden. Whatever it was that made so many Cherokees headstrong had somehow missed getting into Ina's gene pool. She was a quiet, compliant woman who never gave her husband any lip—not in public, anyway.

Greer kicked at a branch of a forsythia bush overhanging the porch with the sharp toe of his Western boot, creating a shower of yellow blossoms. "Listen to me. She's just a silly woman. Ignore her. She can't do you any real harm. You want to know what will really destroy Eagle Rock? Lack of money. We need a park with a community building for meetings—

someplace we can all come together, like a family. We could hold seminars—"

"Don't start with that seminar shit again!"

"—or whatever," Dell amended quickly. "We can decide on the details later. Right now, you have to make more tapes and I'll find more markets for them."

"Pah!" Agasuyed stared into the blackjack oaks at the edge of the yard. His moon face wore a mulish expression. "My father and grandfather were powerful medicine men and they never heard of tapes. Tell me, what can your tapes do against witchcraft? *She* has tapes. No. We have to get back the old ways."

Greer was sick and tired of hearing about the old ways that obsessed Agasuyed, who'd had a series of visions in which the spirit of a long-dead Cherokee peace chief instructed him in the wisdom of the ancients and told him to pass it on to his followers.

Did Agasuyed really think he could turn back the clock? Maybe the man's arteries were so clogged with fat it was preventing enough oxygen getting to his brain. Sometimes Greer suspected that Agasuyed was as crazy as his ex-wife with her medicine cards and vision quests.

When they'd lived in California, Talia had started hanging out with a nutty broad who advertised herself as a channel for some Babylonian noble who'd lived in Old Testament times. Greer had ignored Talia's new diversion, thinking she'd grow bored with it. By then, he'd learned that opposing Talia openly merely hardened her resolve. Besides, who could actually *believe* that stuff?

Apparently Talia.

One day she came home all excited about her meeting with

the channeler. The Babylonian noble, speaking through the nutcase, had delivered a message to Talia, told her to go back to her native roots and prepare to teach her people the way to inner peace. She was going to become a *real* Cherokee.

Greer had laughed in her face. He couldn't help it. Hell, Talia might be half-Cherokee, but at that point she'd known no more about traditional Cherokee culture than Greer himself, which was zero. "Didn't you tell me you're part German and Irish with a little French thrown in?" he'd asked.

She'd glared at him. "What's that got to do with anything?"

"You said this Babylonian dude told you to go back to your native roots. How do you know he meant the Cherokee ones? He could've meant the German, the Irish, or the French."

Of course, his reaction had infuriated her. She'd stamped her foot. "Don't be stupid! He meant Cherokee!"

She'd found her great-great-grandfather's name on the original Dawes Commission tribal roll, had sent off for birth and death records, and filled out the paperwork required to enroll as a tribal member. She'd even taken a correspondence course in the Cherokee language and subscribed to the Cherokee Nation's newspaper, poring over every issue when it came in the mail.

Still, Greer had shrugged it off—until Talia had read about the Eagle Rock community and started nagging him to move back to Cherokee County. "Home," she called it because she'd been born there, even though her folks had taken her to California when she was five years old. As for Greer, he'd never set foot in Cherokee County before. He'd met Talia at a symposium on Native American issues at the junior college they'd

both attended. At that point, he'd been only casually interested in his Indian heritage.

Nevertheless, he'd finally agreed to pull up stakes. Actually,
it had been a good time to leave L.A., as he'd gotten himself
in a tight spot at work. He'd borrowed a few thou from his
employer—with every intention of paying it back. Before he
could, though, an auditor had discovered that the funds were
missing and, after an investigation, Greer was called on the
carpet. He was given the option of repaying the money and
resigning or being prosecuted "to the full extent of the law."
Some choice.

They'd had to sell the house to pay back the money, which
had left him minus a job *and* a house. Oklahoma seemed as
good a place as any to start over, so they'd bought a couple of
acres in Eagle Rock and moved in a mobile home. If he could
have foreseen what would happen, he wouldn't have fallen in
with Talia's plans so easily. Now his ex-wife owned one of the
acres *and* the mobile home.

Greer had set up a little travel trailer on his acre. And little was the operative word. He slept on a narrow couch and
had to straddle the toilet to take a shower. It galled him to
look out his window and see Talia's seventy-footer surrounded by petunias, impatiens, and begonias, with a big
vegetable and herb garden in back. It looked so damned *per-
manent.*

But then almost everything about Talia galled him these
days. And with Agasuyed refusing to cooperate with his plans,
Eagle Rock wasn't all that much fun anymore, either. Even the
wooded hills ringing the small valley and the slower pace of
life in Cherokee County, which had charmed him at first, were
starting to get on his nerves.

When he'd met Agasuyed, who'd turned out to be a real Cherokee medicine man instead of the slick-tongued charlatan Greer had expected, he'd had high hopes. Almost immediately, he began to figure ways he could cash in on Agasuyed's authenticity. He'd made tapes of Agasuyed talking about the old Cherokee religion and way of life, relating some of his visions, and chanting prayers in Cherokee. The tapes were selling like computer chips in California's New Age and feminist bookstores—as were Talia's tapes. She advertised herself as a "spirit caller," which was what she claimed the ancient Cherokees had called conjurers. Who knew?

At any rate, since Greer got half the net profits from Agasuyed's tapes, the opportunity for making big money was there—people would flock to any bizarre spiritual guru nowadays, the kookier, the better. But he couldn't do it without Agasuyed's cooperation. He needed a truckload of blank tapes and a professional-quality dubbing machine. He needed new tapes to market on a regular basis, not to mention money for postage and brochures for a direct mail campaign to widen the customer base. And what was Agasuyed doing? Balking because a woman had wounded his pride.

"Look," Greer said, "forget about Talia. We'll go for a walk in the woods." He'd have to pick the damned ticks off himself afterward, but Agasuyed liked being in the woods. "You can take your shotgun. Maybe we'll see a squirrel."

Agasuyed struggled to his feet and went into the house without a word. What in thunder is he doing now? Greer wondered. Had he been dismissed? Or had Agasuyed gone after his shotgun?—he hadn't shut the door. Greer stepped off the porch, hitched his jeans up over his hipbones, tossed his toothpick into the forsythia bush, and gazed out over

Eagle Rock as he waited beneath a webworm-infested elm tree.

Mobile homes and a few small houses were scattered over what had been the two-hundred-acre Beaver farm. Each dwelling was surrounded by one to three acres of native grasses, trees, and wildflowers. A narrow, graveled road wound through the settlement. Except for the mobile homes, it could have been a Norman Rockwell painting. But constantly having to deal with Agasuyed's inflated ego was beginning to outweigh the rustic beauty of the place.

A few minutes later, Agasuyed came out of his house carrying a small cloth-wrapped bundle but no gun. He lumbered across the yard, ignoring Greer completely.

"Where're you going?"

"Woods."

When Dell started to follow him, Agasuyed halted abruptly and turned around. "I'm going to make medicine. *Tla yi-go-li:-g'.*" He turned and walked into the trees.

Greer recognized *that* word. Agasuyed ended most of their conversations with it. *Tla yi-go-li:-g'* meant goodbye—get lost, buzz off. *Now* he'd been dismissed.

"Hey! We haven't finished talking business."

Agasuyed paused, half-hidden in the shade of giant trees. "*This* is my business. If you can't drive your wife away from here, I will. *Tla yi-go-li:-g'*!"

Greer stewed. The fool was fixated on Talia. Thought he could run her off with Cherokee medicine.

Lotsa luck, fat man.

Greer started home, careful to detour around a big red ant hill in the middle of Agasuyed's front yard.

"Dell?"

He was startled by Ina's soft voice. He hadn't heard her coming. Quietest blamed woman he'd ever met. She was standing at the end of the porch, in front of the Beavers' Chevrolet sedan, a hoe in one hand, looking troubled.

He turned around, walked back toward her. "Hey there, Ina. How you doin'?"

"Real good." He waited for her to say what was on her mind. You had to let Ina do things at her own speed.

In contrast to her husband, she was nothing much but skin and bones, her hair cropped short, bowl fashion, her dark complexion roughened by sun and wind. Ina wasn't much over five feet tall—Greer figured she could be blown away by a good stiff breeze. Worked like a draft horse, though. Agasuyed had done far better than Greer at picking a wife, Greer had to give him that. He stepped closer to better hear her quiet words.

"It's only—well, I'm worried about Agasuyed," she murmured.

"He feeling poorly?" He tried to sound concerned, but at the moment he was so mad at Agasuyed, he wouldn't mind if the man suffered a little.

"No, and that can be a problem, the doctor said. He's got high blood pressure. Sometimes you don't even know you have it till a blood vessel busts."

Greer knew that Agasuyed had recently visited a medical doctor at the Indian hospital. Nothing important, just a checkup, he'd said. He'd told Greer to keep it quiet, his followers might wonder why a medicine man needed a medical doctor. But Greer doubted anybody in the community would turn a hair—most traditional Cherokees subscribed to both kinds of medicine.

The high blood pressure diagnosis was no surprise to Greer, either, and he'd bet the man's cholesterol levels were off the chart. Agasuyed's diet contained way too much fat and sugar. When Ina cooked healthy, he'd eat it, but then he'd sneak off later and go to town for a steak sandwich and fries with a big strawberry malt. A mere mid-afternoon snack to Agasuyed. The man was at least seventy pounds overweight and counting.

"Did the doctor give him pills?" Greer asked.

Ina nodded.

"Is he taking them?"

She fingered the rounded end of the hoe handle and nodded again. "I make sure of that. But he gets so worked up about Talia, I'm afraid he'll have a stroke. He's not sleeping well, for one thing." She shifted the hoe to her other hand. Her black eyes were like polished flint, sharp enough to pierce skin. "I don't understand Talia, Dell. Why does she want to stay where she's not welcome?"

Dell stifled his impatience at the futility of the conversation. Ina just needed a sounding board. "I'm the last person who'd know the answer to that."

"But you were her husband."

"Yeah, and I never did figure Talia out. I can tell you one thing. The more you try to push her, the harder she digs in her heels."

She almost smiled. "Like Agasuyed." She sobered. "He's angry because those women go to Talia now for readings and herbs. I try to tell him to ignore them, but he won't listen to me. I thought maybe you could talk to him."

Bloody hell. What did she think he'd been trying to do for weeks? Did she really imagine Agasuyed would take advice from *him*? "Sure thing, Ina. Don't you worry about it."

"Thank you, Dell," she said softly.

"Don't mention it, Ina."

He shrugged off Ina's request before she was out of sight. But Ina was right about one thing. Talia kept Agasuyed so riled up, he could drop dead any minute, thereby killing Greer's moneymaking schemes as well.

But talking to Agasuyed again would be so much wasted breath. And Dell had tried reasoning with Talia. When that had failed, he'd tried to scare her, saying he couldn't be responsible for what some of her neighbors might do if she didn't leave. Neither tactic had worked.

Greer pondered the problem all the way back to his trailer, where he finally faced facts. One way or another, Talia had to go.

Ha! Now you are brought down.
Ha! There shall be left no more than a trace upon the ground
where you have been.

3

As Molly stepped out of her Honda at the Indian Baptist Church, she saw her grandmother and another woman arranging covered dishes on a long table. She glanced back at her '79 Civic, which had developed a troublesome knock on the drive from her apartment. She hoped it would run until she could get it to a mechanic.

The church, a square white structure with a bell tower, fronted on Willis Road, the country road leading to Park Hill and the Cherokee Heritage Center.

The crowd milling around beneath the trees next to the church looked to number about a hundred.

Eva glanced up over her wire-framed eyeglasses, saw Molly and waved.

Even though Molly had done her laundry Saturday afternoon and now had clean jeans, she was glad she'd dug through her closet and found a yellow cotton dress, a gift from Eva on her last birthday; she didn't see a single woman wearing pants. Even Natalie, who was talking to Talia Wind, had put on a skirt—purple with big white polka dots—for the occasion. It was the first time Molly had seen her in anything but jeans or shorts.

Molly reached Eva and hugged her. As always, Eva stepped back and peered up at Molly from a height of barely five feet, her black eyes examining Molly soberly through her spectacles. Her button-down-the-front green-and-white-checked dress looked a size too large for her. Molly's uneasiness about her grandmother returned. She wondered if Eva had lost weight.

Before Eva could ask, Molly said, "Yes, Grandmother, I'm taking good care of myself."

Eva looked doubtful, but she let it go. "Sorry you couldn't make it for services."

"I overslept," Molly said. D.J. hadn't left her apartment until ten-thirty that morning, but she didn't think her grandmother needed to know that.

"Well . . ." Eva looked her up and down. "I reckon you needed your rest. You look right pretty in that dress."

"Thank you, Grandmother. Now, you want to explain why it was so important for me to be here?"

"I don't see enough of you."

"And?"

Eva's expression turned grave. "I have something to tell you. . . ." She looked around sharply as middle-aged Opal Trynor, a neighbor of Eva's in Park Hill, walked up to the table and deposited a platter of steaming, crusty fried chicken. A mouthwatering smell floated past Molly's nose, making her feel a little faint. She'd had no time for breakfast.

"Hi, Molly," Opal greeted her. "Haven't seen you in a while. You doing okay?"

"Great," Molly told her.

Opal turned to Eva. "I don't think we have enough silverware for everybody."

"There're a bunch of plastic forks and spoons in the church kitchen," Eva told her. "Second drawer to the right of the sink. Clear at the back." Opal trotted away.

Molly was still thinking about the troubled expression Eva had worn before they'd been interrupted. "You were saying, Grandmother . . ."

Eva waved a dismissive hand. "This isn't a good time. We can talk later."

"You look like you've lost weight," Molly persisted. "That dress is hanging on you. You aren't sick, are you?" Eva had always been in good health, but she *was* nearly seventy-seven years old. Molly could not bear to think of losing the woman who'd raised her, who'd always been the anchor for her life.

"Mercy, no, child," Eva said impatiently. "And I haven't lost weight, either. This dress was always too big for me. What I have to tell you has nothing to do with me."

"Then—"

Eva cut her off. "We'll talk later."

Molly knew that tone. She let it drop. "What can I do to help?"

"Not a thing." Eva brushed at a strand of gray hair that had escaped the knot on top of her head. "Mercy, it's going to be a scorcher. You go get yourself a folding chair from that stack over there and sit down under a shade tree till we're ready to eat."

Reassured as to Eva's health, Molly didn't argue. Judging by the number of women she'd seen coming from the back of the church building carrying food, Eva had plenty of help. And if she hung around that table much longer, she was going to lose control and snarf down a chicken leg and some of those baked beans with the bacon strips on top, before anybody had a chance to say grace.

Molly picked up a folding chair and carried it toward the area where she'd seen Natalie and her aunt earlier. She spotted them, engaged in an animated conversation, standing in the same place as before. They'd been joined by Natalie's brother, Ridge, who'd remained in Tahlequah after leaving the university, and a young woman whom Molly recognized as a fellow employee of Ridge's at the Native American Research Library.

The library was housed in an old stone building on the outskirts of Tahlequah but, until recently, the building had stood vacant for years. It had been built in the early 1800s by the Cherokee Nation to provide additional jail space because they'd underestimated the number of cells they'd need when they built the Cherokee Nation prison facing Cherokee Square. The building hadn't been used as a jail since 1907, the year Oklahoma became a state.

When Molly was growing up in Cherokee County, kids had scared themselves and each other with stories about the haunted old jail on the outskirts of town. A predictable outcome, given the building's isolated location, surrounded by underbrush, and the fact that it was abandoned, its windows boarded up.

A few years ago, the Dowell family, who acquired the building when they purchased the two hundred acres adjacent to it, had donated it to a private foundation. The Dowells had built a big automobile dealership and repair and bodyshops on the adjoining land.

The foundation had restored the old jail and turned it into a lending and research library. Since then, the library had received several collections of books and manuscripts written by or dealing with Native Americans, mainly Cherokees. It was gaining a reputation as an important depository of Cherokee research materials.

Since almost everybody was standing, Molly propped her chair against a tree. Natalie saw her and called, "Molly! Hi." She gestured for Molly to join the little group.

Molly greeted Natalie, Ridge, and Talia Wind and was introduced to Deana Cloud, the other library employee.

"Are you related to Kurt Cloud?" Molly asked.

"He's my brother." Deana made a face. And well she might, Molly thought. Kurt Cloud had been in trouble with the law several times since Molly had moved back to Tahlequah—for possession, distribution, and breaking and entering. The few times Molly had seen Kurt, his acne-scarred face had been pulled down in an angry, sullen expression. He might as well have had "Don't mess with me" tattooed on his forehead.

Deana Cloud, who looked to be about Natalie's age, was short with a square face and average build, the sort of girl you'd pass on the street without noticing, except for one thing. She had very large breasts, which she did nothing to minimize. They thrust proudly against the soft material of her low-necked blouse. Size D, Molly thought, wishing

Mother Nature had done a more equal job of apportioning feminine attributes. Deana's frequent glances at Ridge were admiring, while Ridge's attitude toward her seemed warily friendly.

Easy to understand Deana's attraction to Ridge, though. Ridge was twenty-two, two years older than Natalie. In jeans and black Western-style shirt, he was handsome enough to be a Hollywood leading man. If he were the hero of a romance novel, his tan face would have been described as craggy, his easygoing smile, which exposed perfectly even white teeth, as dazzling.

Talia Wind, a tall woman in a flowing, blue silk caftan decorated with a giant red-and-green-beaded feather that curled over one breast and down to her thigh, reminded Molly of the 1940s Hollywood actress Dorothy Lamour, the sarong girl, whose old movies were occasionally shown on late-night television. Talia's thick, silver-streaked black hair fell to her shoulder blades and was swept away from her face in front and held in place with red-beaded combs. Her brown eyes were lively and intelligent. She had the serene, confident look of a woman who was thoroughly at ease with herself and her opinions.

"I don't mean to interrupt a private conversation," Molly said. "You all seemed engrossed in what you were saying."

"We were," Natalie said, "but it's not private." She looked at her aunt, who had been gazing over Natalie's shoulder at a tall, attractive man standing with two other men a few feet away.

"Aunt Talia?" Natalie said.

Talia turned back to her niece. "Yes?"

"I was telling Molly that she wasn't interrupting anything private."

"Not at all." Talia touched the small crystal strung on a silver chain around her neck. Molly knew that New Agers were into crystals, but then Cherokee priests in the old days had also used them to conjure with. When crystals weren't available, they'd used stones or beads.

"Aunt Talia's going to spend the night in the library and try to contact Ulenahiha," Ridge said.

Deana giggled at Molly's blank expression. "Ulenahiha's our library ghost," she clarified.

"Really?" Molly was at a loss for an intelligent response. She finally came up with, "I've always heard the old jail was haunted, but I never knew the ghost had a name."

Nonetheless, her doubt must have been written on her face. "Are you a disbeliever?" Talia Wind inquired with a placid smile. Her voice had a melodic, hypnotic quality. Glancing away from Molly, Talia looked once more at the tall man behind Natalie. The man smiled at Talia, who flashed him a return smile before looking back at Molly. She caressed her crystal.

"In ghosts?" Molly responded to Talia's question, then hesitated. She'd just caught sight of the minister, Dan McCall, from the corner of her eye. In his mid-forties, McCall, who had grayed prematurely, had longish white hair with a sweeping TV-preacher pompadour. As far as Molly knew, he had no Indian blood. He'd been sent to Park Hill by a large congregation in Oklahoma City, the Indian Baptist Church being considered a mission outpost.

McCall had been wandering through the crowd, greeting people. Now, he stopped a few feet behind Talia, blatantly eavesdropping on the conversation. Hands clasped behind his back, he affected a nonchalant pose as he gazed down at the polished toe of his black shoes. Because of where he stood, the others couldn't see him as Molly could.

"I'm not sure," Molly finished judiciously. "I've never seen a ghost myself."

"Few people have," Talia said. "We live in a materialistic age. American culture has made sure most of us are not attuned to the spirit world and, therefore, get only rare, brief intimations of its existence." The implication was that *she*, on the other hand, was intimately familiar with that world.

The preacher shook his head sadly. Molly could imagine him reporting to his sponsoring congregation concerning the heathen superstitions he had to do battle with. Unlike the former preacher, who was part-Cherokee, McCall wasn't tolerant of the old Cherokee traditions.

"I never got *any* intimations," said Deana, "until I went to work at the library. I didn't even *believe* in ghosts, but lately Ulenahiha practically slaps you in the face with his existence."

"The library's ghost is very aggressive," Talia observed, with an approving nod for Deana. "Oh, I don't mean he's violent. I should have said he's persistent. He wants to be released to find peace in the Nightland, like all dead Cherokees, but for some reason he's trapped in this world."

Molly saw McCall heave a deep, silent sigh. She turned to Deana. "How do you know the ghost's name is Ulenahiha?" For that matter, how could they be sure he was Cherokee?

"He told us," Deana said, glancing up at Ridge. The temperature was in the nineties, and tiny beads of perspiration had broken out on his upper lip.

Molly was intrigued in spite of her reluctance to take this ghost story seriously. "You actually *heard* him?"

Ridge pulled a handkerchief from his hip pocket and wiped away the perspiration. "He didn't *say* his name. He put it in the computer."

Molly laughed. "You're making this up."

"No, I'm not," Ridge said. "I swear. See, one morning a couple of weeks ago I went to work and tried to pull up the file I'd worked on the day before, but it wasn't there. I looked through all the directories, but it was gone. I figured I was in big trouble, because that file contained important library records. We had to call in a computer serviceman, and he found a file labeled 'Ulenahiha.'"

"It means in Cherokee to lose one's way," Talia inserted.

Ridge nodded. "None of us had ever heard of a file by that name, but when we pulled it up, it was the lost file. The ghost had relabeled it—with what we took to be his name. Anyway, that's what we call him."

A computer-literate ghost? Molly mused.

"Since then, we've heard him several times," Deana added. "Not words really, but other sounds—like somebody's moving chairs across the floor downstairs in the half-basement where we have our meeting room and kitchen. A week ago about closing time, we heard that noise, like chairs scraping across the concrete floor. It sounded like six or seven people were down there. We were all afraid to go down—all except Ridge, that is."

"Nobody was in the basement," Ridge went on. "We knew that already, but somebody had to look. We couldn't remember where the chairs were before, so we couldn't tell if they'd been moved. But we're sure it was Ulenahiha reminding us that he's still there. Once, we left a tape recorder running in the basement at night to see if we could pick up anything."

"And did you?" Molly asked.

Ridge looked faintly disappointed. "More scraping noises and what sounded like soft footsteps in the background. But that's all."

Talia ran the crystal over her bottom lip, then let it drop between her breasts. "These manifestations have increased alarmingly just in the last two or three weeks."

As the others talked about Ulenahiha, Molly could still see McCall from the corner of her eye. The preacher's expression, his very stance, had become one of increasing disapproval.

"I've only worked at the library for three weeks," Deana said, "and the second day I was there, I had to work late." She sounded breathless with the memory. "Nobody told me the place was haunted. About dark, I heard creaking noises downstairs. It was scary, but I convinced myself it was just the old building settling. Then, I heard what sounded like chains being dragged across the floor." She gave a nervous little laugh, then slapped her palms together, sliding one across the other. "Thought I'd die! I shot off my chair and was out of there in two seconds flat!"

"Tell Molly about seeing the ghost in the glass door, Ridge," Natalie urged.

"*I* haven't seen him," Ridge corrected, tucking his handkerchief into a shirt pocket, "but Alice, our reference librarian, has seen Ulenahiha's reflection in a glass door that separates the reference room from the rest of the library. When you're sitting at the desk just outside that room, the door is in front of you and to the right. Alice looked up from the computer and saw a man's reflection in the glass. It was sort of hazy, like he was standing in smoke. But she could tell he was bare-chested and wore a necklace with what looked like an eagle feather hanging from it."

"When she turned around, no one was there," Deana added, "and when she looked back at the glass, the reflection was gone, too." She shook her head. "It's getting so we're all about half-afraid to be there alone, even in broad daylight."

"I don't think he means to harm you," Talia said calmly, "but this is a very determined ghost."

"Determined?" Molly queried.

"He wants to be released from his imprisonment here."

"And Aunt Talia's going to help him," Natalie said.

"How?" Molly asked.

Two fine lines etched themselves into Talia's smooth brow. "That is, indeed, the question. I may first have to find out why he's trapped here. It's possible he was a prisoner in that building when it was a jail. Perhaps he was wrongly convicted of a crime and wants his name cleared. It's even possible that he was murdered and his spirit can't rest until the murder is avenged."

"But if he was murdered," Natalie put in, "the murderer must be dead, too, by this time."

Talia nodded gravely, acknowledging the point. "In which case, exposing the identity of the true murderer might be enough to free the ghost. Or it may only take the proper medicine ceremony to release him." All at once, she stiffened, sensing the presence behind her and turned. "Why, hello, Reverend McCall."

"Miss Wind." He hesitated, then stepped forward and exchanged greetings with the others.

"You preached a fine sermon this morning," Talia said.

"Thank you, ma'am."

"I am always amazed at the way you can quote Scripture from memory. Do you have the entire Bible memorized?"

McCall smiled. "Not quite, but a Scripture did come to mind as I listened to your conversation just now." He glanced around the group with an expression of gentle benevolence, like a wise adult indulging the fancies of children.

Uh-oh, Molly thought.

"It's from Isaiah," McCall was saying, "'And when they say to you, "Consult the mediums and the spiritists who whisper and mutter," should not a people consult their God? Should they consult the dead on behalf of the living?'"

Talia's arched black brows rose in questioning amusement. "What was Isaiah's answer?"

McCall chuckled, although Molly thought it sounded fake. "The questions were rhetorical because the answer was obvious."

"I seem to recall," Talia said, cradling her crystal in one hand, "that God's anointed, King Saul, once consulted a witch and asked her to contact the dead prophet Samuel. Which she did, if I'm not mistaken." Her eyes held McCall's, dancing a challenge.

She's enjoying this, Molly thought, and for the first time got an inkling of why Talia refused to leave Eagle Rock. Opposition seemed to energize her.

Natalie and Deana exchanged uneasy looks and Ridge

shuffled his feet uncomfortably. Molly glanced at the minister and caught a tensing of his shoulders in the black suit jacket.

"You are referring to the witch of Endor," said McCall. He seemed to be struggling to maintain a tolerant tone. "And that wasn't the first time Saul went against God's law. In fact, if you'll read further in that Scripture, you'll find that Samuel came out of the spirit world to tell Saul that God had departed from him and had become his adversary. Because of Saul's sins, God gave the kingdom to David instead of to one of Saul's descendants."

"But Saul tried to kill David," Talia said. "Surely that was the sin that cost him the kingdom."

"The attempts on David's life occurred *after* God had chosen David to succeed to the throne. It merely added to Saul's accumulation of sins," McCall insisted, "not the least of which was consulting a sorceress. The Old Testament law was perfectly clear on the subject of witchcraft, Miss Wind. You can read it for yourself in Exodus. 'You shall not allow a sorceress to live.' "

Right back at you, Molly thought.

McCall's gaze held Talia's unwaveringly. Her challenge had been accepted and he was issuing one of his own.

After a second's hesitation, Talia laughed. "I believe that law also sanctioned the stoning of rebellious children. Aren't you glad *we* don't live under that old legalistic system, Reverend? The New Testament is based on grace and love."

McCall gave her a smug little smile, as though Talia had stepped into a trap. He pounced. "Surely you're familiar with the apostle Paul's words in the New Testament book of Galatians, Miss Wind. In the fifth chapter, verses nineteen and following, the deeds of the flesh are listed. You'll find sorcery there along with immorality and idolatry. 'Those who practice such things shall not inherit the kingdom of God.'"

Talia's serenity slipped a little. "Doesn't the New Testament teach us not to judge one another?"

"Indeed it does. But I'm not judging you."

Talia shrugged, as though determined to appear untouched by the preacher's criticism. She glanced toward the tall man she'd been watching before the minister had joined the group just as a woman walked up, put her arm through the man's and led him away. The woman looked back over her shoulder and her gaze locked with Talia's. Her expression was one of pure hatred.

Talia flushed and looked away hastily. "If you're not judging me, Reverend McCall, what do you call it?"

"Teaching, Miss Wind."

Talia laughed. "A thorn by any other name is still a thorn."

A little muscle twitched next to the minister's mouth. "I am merely repeating Paul's words. That's my profession, and my calling. If you doubt what I say, you can look it up for yourself." Having scored a point off Talia, he touched the tips of his fingers together, tent-fashion, and his expression became one of benediction. His duty here had been discharged. He looked past Talia toward the back of the church. "Ah, it appears the ladies are ready to serve. It's time for me to ask God's blessing on the food. Good day." He smiled around the circle of faces and walked briskly toward the tables where the food was laid out.

Thoughtfully, Talia watched him leave, her dark brows drawn together tightly.

"Whew!" breathed Ridge, pulling out his handkerchief again to wipe sweat off his brow. "Did you see how red his neck got? He was *mad.*"

"You shouldn't let him bait you, Aunt Talia," Natalie said.

From Molly's viewpoint, Talia had been baiting the preacher. And, mostly, she had liked doing it. Molly wondered now if Talia had been aware of the preacher's presence behind her all along. And then Molly wondered if Talia made a point of baiting Agasuyed Beaver, too. It might explain Beaver's intense opposition to her, even more than their religious differences.

Talia continued to gaze after McCall. "How sad," she said finally. "McCall is an intelligent man, but he seems to take any disagreement with his philosophy as a personal affront."

"Maybe you shouldn't argue with him on his own ground," Ridge suggested.

"I wasn't arguing," Talia corrected him. "I was having a friendly debate."

A thorn by any other name, Molly thought. It had been obvious that the preacher didn't see the exchange as friendly. And Molly wasn't sure that Talia did, either. She thought McCall had gotten under Talia's skin there at the end.

"It's unfortunate," Talia mused, "that so many people have closed their minds to the spiritual power available to all of us."

But the words had an edge to them.

You have now put it into a crevice in a high mountain,
that it may never find the way back.

4

Eva led Molly away from the table. They carried paper plates laden with good country cooking and large Styrofoam cups of iced tea.

Catching sight of the tall man who had smiled at Talia and the woman who had led him away, Molly said, "Grandmother, who is that man sitting with the minister's group? He's wearing a yellow shirt."

Eva paused to let her gaze find the man. "That's Josh Rollins. He's one of our deacons."

"The name's sort of familiar."

"He's only been here a year or so. Built that nice new restaurant north of town."

"Is that his wife sitting beside him?"

"Yes, that's Belinda. Why?"

"Just curious."

Eva walked on ahead of Molly. "I got us a good spot," she

called over her shoulder. She headed for a cottonwood tree which stood at the edge of the churchyard just outside the fence surrounding a small family cemetery, where no new graves had been added for as long as Molly could remember. Some of the stones had crumbled to rubble, others had fallen or been knocked over. In spite of the graves, it presented a peaceful scene, the new spring grass shaded by venerable old trees.

Eva had previously placed two folding chairs in the shade, facing the cemetery. Their plates cradled in their laps, they removed the lids from their tea and set the cups on the grass beside them.

It had not escaped Molly's notice that Eva had chosen a spot away from the crowd and had deliberately positioned the chairs with their backs to the church and anybody who might have thought of joining them.

Now, Molly thought, she's going to tell me why she wanted me here today. A feeling of trepidation passed through her, like storm clouds moving in, and she had an illogical impulse to stop whatever Eva was going to tell her before the words were out. Could anything so difficult for Eva to say be good? But Molly shook off the feeling and waited for Eva to speak.

Instead of going straight to the point, Eva looked toward the cemetery and said, "I saw you talking to that Talia Wind woman." At least, Molly didn't *think* Talia was the point, even though there was certainly disapproval in Eva's tone.

"She's Natalie's aunt," Molly said. "You remember Natalie, the girl who works for me part-time."

Eva nodded. "I saw her there, too. And her brother and some other girl." She picked up a chicken breast with two hands, took a bite, laid it down, and wiped the grease off her chin with a paper napkin. She looked over at Molly. "And the preacher."

Molly suspected most of the crowd had watched the conversation between Talia and the minister. "He heard us talking about the Native American Research Library's ghost," Molly said. When Eva didn't respond, Molly sampled her crusty chicken leg and gave silent thanks for the woman who'd prepared it, whoever she might be. Then she took a bite of a homemade clover leaf roll dripping with melted butter and washed it down with a cold swallow of tea. "Talia Wind is going to spend the night at the library and try to make contact with the ghost," Molly went on. "Talia says he's restless and wants to go to the Nightland, but for some reason he's trapped here."

Eva studied her sharply, as though to discover if Molly was teasing her. She clicked her tongue against her teeth in disapproval.

"You don't believe in ghosts?" Molly asked.

"It's Talia Wind I'm talking about right now. I don't like that woman," Eva replied, skirting a direct answer to Molly's question. But Molly thought she knew the answer. Eva rarely mentioned night walkers or night goers, Cherokee ghosts, but when she did it was with mingled fear and respect.

"Reverend McCall seems to agree with you."

"Of course he does," Eva said, scowling. "I don't know why that woman wants to show her face in this church. But lately, a couple Sundays a month, you can count on her turning up."

Molly wondered if Deacon Rollins had anything to do with Talia's attendance.

"She always sits near the front, too," Eva was saying. "It's like she's taunting the Reverend." She glanced around them to see if anyone was close enough to overhear. Satisfied that no one was, she went on. "I've noticed he preaches louder and prays longer when she's in the audience. The preacher has strict ideas about mixing superstition with doctrine."

"But doesn't he consider visiting a medicine man superstition?" Molly asked as she scooped up a spoonful of baked beans flavored with molasses and ketchup and brown sugar. "I know you and other members of this church have used a medicine man and would again. How does the preacher handle that?"

Eva frowned at her. "This preacher doesn't understand our ways. But he doesn't have to know everything about people's private lives. We just don't talk about things like that in front of him. It's our way of showing respect for his opinions. Not like Talia Wind. Why, she waves all that conjuring mumbo-jumbo in his face. You'd think she'd at least have the decency not to wear that crystal around her neck in church."

"Talia's philosophy seems to be live and let live."

"Well, it isn't the preacher's. Did the two of 'em have words?"

"In a civilized sort of way. Reverend McCall could quote more Scripture than Talia, so I think he came out ahead."

Eva nodded in approval. "Good for him. Maybe she'll find herself another church where she can go and stir up trouble. She's not even a member here, you know."

"No, I didn't know that," Molly said, not really surprised. Talia probably considered herself a member-at-large in all religions, and wouldn't favor one over the other by making her membership official.

Molly finished off the chicken leg and started on her

scrambled eggs and wild onions. This year they'd even had scrambled egg substitute and wild onions for the cholesterol-conscious, but Molly had chosen the real thing.

"If Talia was a member, the preacher might have called a meeting and had her de-churched before now."

"De-churched?" The term was new to Molly.

"Disfellowshipped. That's when they announce from the pulpit that somebody has rejected God's way to serve the devil and all the other members are supposed to shun 'em."

"What if the person keeps coming to church, anyway?"

"I don't know. I guess some of the men would escort 'em right out again. Or maybe they'd just ignore 'em."

"When was the last time you heard of somebody being disfellowshipped?"

"I haven't seen it in—oh, must be thirty years. People have gotten more liberal in their thinking. It'd take something mighty serious today, and I'm not sure that's all to the good, either. In my younger days, people knew the line between right and wrong."

In some ways, life must have been easier then, Molly thought. You might step over the line, but you knew exactly when you'd done it.

"If Talia would keep all her talk about spirits and visions for the folks out at Eagle Rock, it'd be one thing," Eva went on, "but I reckon the preacher thinks she's coming in here and trying to entice good Christians onto the devil's pathway. You can't get much more serious than that."

Molly dabbed at her mouth with a napkin. "It does seem," she mused, "that Talia would have enough opposition from Agasuyed Beaver without inviting more of it from Reverend McCall."

Eva nodded. "Exactly what I was thinking. Opal Trynor's a good friend of Ina Beaver, and she says Agasuyed is madder than a hornet because Talia's still at Eagle Rock. He's bound and determined to force her out."

"Natalie says that's not going to happen. It's a point of honor with Talia."

"Honor, bah! It's downright mulishness." Eva took a bite of scrambled eggs. They ate in silence for a few moments, Eva seeming to have finally exhausted the subject of Talia Wind.

After a while, Molly asked, "So, what was it you wanted to tell me, Grandmother?"

Eva appeared about to open her mouth, but then she hesitated, turning to gaze at the riot of red blossoms on the wild rose bush entwined in the cemetery's fence. After a long moment, her eyes came back to Molly's, and they held distress.

Alarmed, Molly asked, "What is it, Grandmother?"

Eva put down her fork and sighed. "Been trying for days to figure out how to tell you. Reckon there's only one way, plain and quick." She took a deep breath as if she would have to force the next words out against their will. "I heard from your father last week."

The words hung suspended in the air between them like weightless blobs. There was an instant when Molly could not comprehend them, as if Eva had spoken in a foreign tongue. Then, the meaning hit her like a fist. She couldn't have been more shocked if Eva had said she'd heard from Molly's long-dead mother, Josephine. For a few moments, Molly was speechless, able only to gape at Eva while a swarm of conflicting emotions threatened to choke her. She grabbed her tea and gulped down a mouthful.

Eva leaned toward her. "Maybe I shouldn't have hit you

with it like that, only I couldn't put it off any longer. You all right?"

Molly went into a fit of coughing. A drop of tea had gone down the wrong way. Eva patted her on the back, murmuring sympathetically.

When she could get her breath, Molly choked out, "I'm fine."

"Uh-huh." Obviously Eva didn't believe her.

Molly tried to assimilate the news that her father had returned. It was a concept she had trouble getting her mind around.

When she was growing up, she would have given anything to have a father, but she'd stopped dreaming that dream years ago. She sorted through a maze of questions and picked one. "Did he come to your house or what?"

"He phoned."

"Where from?"

"He didn't say, but he must be around here somewhere— or on the way. He wants to see you."

Molly had pretty much figured that out already. Why else would he have contacted Eva, his former mother-in-law? Thank goodness, Molly told herself, he hadn't called *her* out of the blue. Robert Bearpaw had deserted his family when Molly was four years old, and she hadn't heard from him since then. As Eva had never kept any pictures of him around, Molly couldn't even remember what he looked like. She doubted she would know him if he stood right in front of her. She realized in that moment, that when she thought of him at all, she thought of him as dead. Why else would she never have heard from him in all those years?

The flood of emotions seemed to have crystallized into only one. Anger.

"Why?"

Eva sighed. "Why what?"

"Why does he want to see me?"

"You're his daughter."

"Oh, did he suddenly remember that little detail—after more than twenty-five years?" Her voice broke, which angered her even more.

"Well, there was something . . . I—I got the feeling he's not well."

"I hope he doesn't expect me to rush to his bedside!"

Eva just looked at her and shook her head. "That's hurt talking, girl."

"What's wrong with him?"

"He didn't say. He didn't even tell me he was sick—not in so many words. It was just a feeling." She watched Molly wad her napkin, lay it on her plate, and set the plate on the ground.

Oh, God. Infuriated by the tears that had sprung to her eyes, Molly used the hem of her dress to wipe them away. "I wish he'd just stayed gone."

"Well, he didn't."

"Why couldn't he leave well enough alone?"

"You'll have to ask him," Eva said, then at Molly's dark look, added, "if you ever have the chance. He promised he'd wait until you agree, before he comes to see you. But he sounded right determined."

Molly stared at the wild rose bush. How could the serene setting be unchanged while she was attacked by a storm of feelings? "I can't believe this," she murmured.

"Kind of knocked the props out from under me, too. He's going to call again. What should I tell him?"

"Tell him—" Dammit, Molly fumed, why did her voice keep breaking? But at least she now knew why Eva had wanted to tell her there, in private but with a hundred people close by. She had probably expected Molly to throw a fit and thought the audience would deter her.

In fact, Molly *wanted* to throw a fit. She wanted to kick and hurl things and curse the name of Robert Bearpaw, the stranger who was responsible for her very existence. The man who had driven away from a little house in Park Hill that wasn't even standing anymore, without a backward glance. The man who had been living his life somewhere for a quarter century with not a worry for the daughter he'd left behind.

Molly managed to keep these thoughts from spewing from her mouth in a torrent of fury. She cleared her throat. "Tell him I have to think about it. Tell him there's no big hurry. He can just wait till I'm good and ready to give him an answer, after *twenty-five years!* And I'll tell you something, Grandmother. I may *never* be ready. You can tell him that, too!"

"Molly—"

"No, I mean it!" Molly jumped up. "He ran off, left me and Mama—*your daughter*—to fend for ourselves and she couldn't—couldn't cope with it." Molly's mother had committed suicide when Molly was six, though Eva had always maintained that the shooting was accidental. "Now he's sick and wants to come crawling back home." She became aware that her voice had risen and that several people were looking their way. She knew she was going to cry. "I have to leave now, Grandmother."

"But you haven't even had dessert."

"I've lost my appetite."

Eva's lined face crumpled like a piece of paper being wadded in an invisible hand. "Molly, you were a child. You don't know what went on before he left—or since then."

Molly stared at her, blinking back tears. "I can't believe you're defending him!"

"I'm not defending him. I'm just saying that it happened twenty-five years ago." She heaved a sigh. "Holding a grudge hurts the one who holds it more than anybody else." She drew in a big breath of air, as if trying to shrug a heavy weight off her chest. "That's one lesson I've learned in my seventy-six years. Think about it."

"I can't just turn my feelings off like a light switch."

"I know," Eva murmured. After a moment, she said, "I could've killed him myself with my bare hands when he left. But I've had a lot of time to think about it and Rob wasn't the only one at fault in that marriage. There was enough blame to go around."

"So he ran away. Is that how you fix troubled marriages?" And what about *me*, Molly wailed silently.

"You know that's not what I'm saying, Molly. But Josephine was too young to get married in the first place. Echols and me tried to talk to her, but she wouldn't listen. You can't remember, but she wasn't ready to settle down and care for a baby. She still wanted to run around with her friends, like she did in high school. Oh, she loved you, never doubt that. I'm just saying she wasn't hardly more than a child herself."

How ironic, Molly thought. When Molly was growing up, she'd asked questions about her parents, but Eva had never wanted to talk about them. Talking about it will just get us both down in the dumps, Molly, she'd say and then change the subject.

Just now Eva had told Molly more about her mother than in all the years before—only at the moment Molly was in no mood to hear it.

"I know she loved me, Grandmother," Molly said. "And I remember more than you think."

"He loved you, too."

"Oh, really? He sure had a great way of showing it."

Molly's memories of her father were fragmented and hazy. She could remember running to meet him when he came home from work, her father laughing and swinging her up in his arms. "What was the happiest thing that happened to you today, Miss Molly?" he'd ask.

She remembered sitting beside him in the front seat of the car, just the two of them, going to town for ice cream, her father mussing her hair, saying, "I want a double-dip chocolate cone. What do you want, Miss Molly?"

And she remembered his bringing home a part-bulldog puppy he'd found on the side of the road. "Look at that ugly mug," he'd said. "Now, I ask you, doesn't he look like he needs a little girl to take care of him?" She'd named the pup Mugsy, but they couldn't break Mugsy of chasing cars, and she'd only had him a few weeks when he'd been killed by a pickup truck.

It was shortly after that when her father left. She remembered how things changed then, how the shades were pulled, the house dark all the time, her mother lying on the couch, a bottle of whiskey always near at hand.

She remembered being terrified, wondering if her father had died and they weren't telling her.

Later, she remembered spending the night with her grand-parents, thinking it was like all the other nights her mother had left her with them. But the next morning, Eva sat on her bed and told her that her mother had had to go away. It was weeks before she realized her mother was dead and years be-fore she knew Josephine had taken her own life.

She remembered . . .

Or were they merely dreams and not real memories at all?

Whatever they were, Molly slammed a door on them. "I can't talk about this anymore right now, Grandmother. I need to be alone. I'll see you later." The words hurt her throat, as if they were too large for the narrowed passageway, and when she got to the end of them, she was incapable of uttering an-other sound.

Molly turned and ran toward her car without looking back.

You have put it to rest in the Darkening Land,
so that it may never return. Let relief come.

5

By sheer force of will, Molly shoved the Civic into gear and her mind into neutral. She drove by reflex, hardly aware of where she was until she neared Tahlequah's city limits, marked by the Native American Research Library and Dowell's Foreign Car Sales, Automotive Repair, and Body Shop on the county side of the line, where businesses were taxed at a lower rate than within the city.

The knock in the Civic's motor had gotten loud enough to penetrate the self-imposed fog that was keeping thoughts at bay. It sounded like metal striking metal—hard. If she kept driving, with every yard she could be adding dollars to the repair bill which was now clearly inevitable. For all she knew, the car could go up in flames if she didn't stop.

Once she'd focused on the here and now, the thought she'd been keeping at arm's length rushed back.

Her father was alive and wanted to see her.

At one time, she would have greeted the news with joy, but not now. She had long ago resigned herself to the loss of both her parents. Her life would have been so much simpler if he'd left it at that.

What was the happiest thing that happened to you today, Miss Molly? I want a double-dip chocolate cone. What do you want, Miss Molly?

What was she going to do?

She didn't know.

She forced the questions aside. Right now it was the car she had to focus on.

She pulled in behind the library, braked, and turned off the motor. Smoke rose from beneath the car hood. She got out and stared at the hood, but she wouldn't know what to look for if she lifted it. She reached back inside for her purse and keys.

She was four or five miles from her apartment, and her flat barefoot sandals weren't choice walking shoes. She looked toward the highway. There was always the possibility somebody she knew might come along and give her a lift.

She turned her back on the Civic and walked toward town. She was concentrating so hard on *not* thinking about her father and worrying about how much the Honda repair bill would be that she didn't notice the late-model black Lexus parked in front of the foreign car place until she was past it.

The business wasn't open on Sundays, so the Lexus probably belonged to the owner, Rayburn Dowell, whom Molly knew by sight, though she hadn't seen him around town lately. A while back, she'd heard that he'd taken his son into the business with him. She decided to see if she could find him and ask him to pull her Honda over to his shop tomorrow.

The showroom door was locked. She banged on the glass and called, "Anybody in there?"

Seconds later, two men, one of them Rayburn Dowell, who was in his sixties, walked out from between the showroom and the repair garages behind it. The other man was younger, in his early thirties—the son, Molly realized. The two men looked so much alike that the elder could have been the younger grown thirty-some years older. What was left of Rayburn Dowell's auburn hair among the gray was the same color as the younger man's. Both were tall, six feet or slightly more, although the older man's shoulders stooped a little now. Their eyes were the same hazel color, but the father's held a lost expression as he looked at his son, a look that Molly could only describe as helpless.

It was the younger man who came toward her. "May I help you, ma'am?"

"My Honda Civic broke down," Molly told him. "I pulled it in behind the library next door. Do you think you could take a look at it tomorrow?"

"Sure." He stuck out his hand. "I'm Tim Dowell."

"Molly Bearpaw," she said as they shook hands.

"What seems to be the problem with your car?"

"The motor's making a knocking noise."

He nodded. "Uh-oh. Could be serious. What year is it?"

"A '79," Molly said, "and it's got almost a hundred and fifty thousand miles on it."

"Some of those old Civics can go two hundred thousand without a major breakdown. But a knock in the motor . . ." He shook his head. "I don't like the sound of it." He laughed suddenly. "No pun intended."

"Could you let me know what it'll cost to fix it before you do anything?"

"You bet." She took her car key off the ring and handed it to him. He fished a pen and a business card out of his pocket. "Give me your daytime phone number."

As he jotted down the information, Molly became aware that Rayburn Dowell had not moved from the spot where his son had left him. She glanced at him and smiled.

Although he seemed to be looking right at her, his expression didn't change.

Tim Dowell tucked the keys, card, and pen in his pocket. "Where do you live?"

"On Keetowah Street." She gave him the number. "It's not too far to walk."

"Isn't that near where Professor Swope lives?"

"It's exactly where he lives," Molly said. "I rent his garage apartment."

"I know the place, then, and it's a fair piece. I'll take you. Dad and I were going home, anyway." He glanced over his shoulder at his father, who seemed to have put down roots on the spot. He lowered his voice, "I pretty much run the business now, but sometimes Dad forgets. He'll get a bee in his bonnet that he forgot to lock up when he left the office. He can't rest till we come down and check. Last week, I had to bring him out here in the middle of the night. He hasn't worked in his office in months, but he gets confused about time."

"I'm so sorry," Molly said.

He lifted his broad shoulders. "Doc thinks it's Alzheimer's—he's about eliminated everything else. I had to get a woman to keep an eye on him when I'm working. We lost Mom three years ago. In a way, it's a good thing she didn't live to see Dad like he is now. She depended on him a lot. Before I hired a sit-ter for him, he'd wander off and couldn't remember where home was. Has to be told to take a bath and use the toilet." He shook his head unhappily.

"I'm sorry," Molly repeated. What else was there to say?

"Nothing anybody can do," he said stoically. "Well—" He seemed to shake himself and grinned at her. "Let's get you home. My car's out front." He walked back to his father. "Come on, Dad. Everything's locked up good and tight. We're going home now." He grasped his father's arm and led him to-ward the Lexus. Rayburn Dowell came docilely. Molly fol-lowed them.

Tim Dowell unlocked the car, guided his father into the back seat, and secured his seat belt, leaving the front passen-ger seat for Molly. The soft white leather sighed as she sank into it.

"If the repair work on your car is going to take several days," Tim said as they drove away, "I can probably find a loaner for you."

Molly thought about her savings account, which contained four hundred and fifty-some dollars and knew she couldn't afford a rental car. She wasn't even sure she could afford to have the Honda repaired. "Thanks, but I'll manage."

He looked over at her. His face was broad and covered with barely visible freckles. It was a pleasant, friendly face. "There's an '87 Accord been sitting on the used car lot for a month. We took it in as a trade. You might as well be driving it. Won't cost you a thing. It's part of the package."

"That's awfully considerate of you."

"We try to keep our customers happy. Service is our mid-dle name, ma'am."

She smiled. "I'll take you up on that offer then—if you have to keep my car a while. Problem is, I'm not sure the Civic is worth fixing."

"You never know. Let me get one of my mechanics to look at it, see what's wrong, what it'll take to fix it."

They passed the Cherokee tribal office complex on the right; it was flanked by the Cherokee Nation's Talking Leaves Job Corps Center and gift shop.

Glancing toward the main office building, Tim said, "It just came to me—I thought I recognized your name. Don't you work for the Cherokee Nation?"

"Yes, I'm a liaison officer in the major crimes unit—my office is downtown." According to her job description, she was supposed to work with whatever city, county, state, or federal law enforcement agency had jurisdiction when an enrolled Cherokee was involved in a felony, either as victim or as the accused or suspected perpetrator. Provided she was welcome, which she had learned not to count on. Sometimes she had to conduct an independent investigation.

Tim glanced up at the rearview mirror. "You okay back there, Dad?"

The older man muttered something unintelligible. Tim looked at Molly. "One thing about Alzheimer's, there's no pain."

Remembering the lost, confused look on Rayburn Dowell's face back at the dealership, Molly thought Tim was wrong. The emotional and mental pain attached to the flashes of clarity when you realized you didn't know where you were or even who you were must be terrifying.

The silence following Tim's words lasted until Molly spoke. "You said you've had to bring your father to the dealership at night—"

He glanced at her. "A couple of times."

"The library would have been closed. Did you notice anything unusual over there?"

"At the old jail?" He frowned, and then his face cleared and he chuckled. "Oh, you mean the ghost?"

"Or whatever," Molly said, feeling foolish for even mentioning it. "The employees can tell some pretty eerie tales. They, at least, are convinced the place is haunted."

"The old jail has always had that reputation. I remember hearing it when I was in school."

"Yeah, me too."

"I think I remember you. You were a couple of years behind me."

"That's right," Molly said, not wanting to admit that she had no memory of Tim Dowell at all.

After a brief silence, Tim said, "You get a bunch of people who are convinced there's a ghost in residence, they're going to spook each other into imagining things."

"I guess."

Suddenly, Molly felt warmth near her ear. Twisting around, she found Rayburn Dowell's face inches from hers. He was breathing through his mouth and his breath smelled of dentures that needed a good scrubbing. His eyes held the dazed look of illness—or madness.

"He went through the wall." Rayburn Dowell's voice creaked, as though it wasn't used enough to keep it in good working order.

Molly turned aside to avoid his foul breath. She shot a worried look at Tim, who appeared untroubled. He was probably used to his father's incomprehensible conversation.

"What's that, Dad?" Tim asked.

"I saw him. It was night."

"You saw something go through a wall? What night was that?"

"He went through the jail wall."

Tim winked at Molly as though to assure her, he's harmless. "Is that right?" He said it in the indulgent way you'd speak to a child who insists he'd seen an elf.

Rayburn Dowell seemed to have lost the tenuous thread of his thoughts. He sat back in the seat and stared out a window.

"Hey, Dad," Tim said cheerfully, "how's about we have us a big bowl of ice cream when we get home? Would you like that?"

I want a double-dip chocolate cone. What do you want, Miss Molly?

In her mind, Molly suddenly saw her father's face, looking down at her as they drove to Tahlequah for an ice cream treat, fine smile wrinkles fanning from the corners of his eyes. The last time had been only days before he disappeared, or that's how she remembered it. She tried to hold his image in her mind, searched his face for a clue of what was going to happen, though she'd had no way of knowing it then, as if looking for some key to an otherwise indecipherable code.

"You'd like some ice cream, wouldn't you, Dad?" Tim asked. "I think we've got butter brickle."

There was no response from the back seat, which didn't seem to bother Tim. Molly admired the way he appeared able to keep his spirits up in the face of his father's mental deterioration. Many men would have put Rayburn Dowell in a nursing facility, but Tim kept him at home. It had to be hard on him, and it said a lot about his love for his father. As sad as the situation was, Molly almost envied Tim. His father had been there for him when he was growing up, and now that the roles were reversed Tim had willingly become the caregiver. Molly wanted to believe she would have done the same, under those circumstances.

Molly thought of what Eva had said, that Molly's father wasn't well. If that were true, was he too sick to work or even to care for himself? Maybe that's why he'd come back. He could get free medical care at the Indian hospital. Was he hoping his daughter would feel obliged to take him in?

"Here we are," Tim said, scattering Molly's thoughts. He turned into the driveway next to Conrad's house and she got out.

"Thanks for the ride, Mr. Dowell."

"Hey, what's this Mr. Dowell stuff? It's Tim."

"Okay, Tim. Will I hear from you tomorrow?"

"I'll get a mechanic to check out your car first thing. I'll call you as soon as I get his estimate."

"Good, and thanks again." She glanced at the man in the back seat. "Goodbye, Mr. Dowell."

His hazel eyes focused on her. "Who are you?" he asked.

Tim sighed. "Nobody you know, Dad. Catch you later, Molly."

She closed the car door, and Tim backed into the street. Rayburn Dowell peered out at her with a bewildered expression. Once an active, vibrant man, now his mind was slowly slipping away, and he couldn't understand what was happening to him.

She turned and headed down the driveway in the other direction, toward her apartment. Her golden retriever, Homer, saw her and jumped up with his front paws on the fence, barking a gleeful welcome, and tried to shake his tail off.

Conrad Swope, Molly's landlord, a retired history professor, was visiting a brother in Seattle and wouldn't be back for several weeks. Homer was lonely and missed his daily walks with Conrad.

Talia Wind parked beside her mobile home and got out of her car. She'd left a sprinkler hose running in the flower bed, which would be thoroughly soaked by now. She started toward the faucet, then remembered that she was wearing her best silk caftan and didn't want to risk getting it sprayed. She'd turn off the water after she changed clothes.

Thunder grumbled in the distance. Wouldn't you know it? Glancing up at the darkening sky, she wished she'd held off on the watering. Clouds had begun to gather before she left the church and now a cooling breeze had come up. It was going to rain any minute.

She went up the steps to the small, square stoop Dell had built beneath the front door of the mobile home. Opening the storm door, she fitted her key into the lock in the inner door. As she did so, thunder rumbled again and a drop of rain plopped on her arm.

She glanced toward Dell's trailer on the adjoining acre, relieved that he was nowhere in sight. In fact, his car was gone, and she wondered idly where he was. She tried to avoid contact with her ex-husband. Their conversations usually got around to his offering to buy her out if she'd leave Eagle Rock. All she had to do was name her price. Dell always talked as if he was rolling in cash, even when he hardly had two dimes to rub together. She was sure Dell didn't have the money to buy her out, although he might get it from Agasuyed, who wanted her to disappear as much as Dell did. Even Ina, who had once been a friend, now turned away whenever she saw Talia. She could manage to shrug off Dell and Agasuyed, but the change in Ina's attitude hurt her deeply.

In the last three weeks, since she'd been attacked, approaching or leaving her mobile home after dark made her jumpy. Before the attack, she'd often walked around the compound at night. That's what she had been doing when somebody stepped out of the woods behind her, hit her with something hard like a thick limb or a baseball bat, and melted back into the woods. The attacker may have been aiming at her head, but had connected with her right arm instead. She'd staggered forward, barely kept herself from falling, and by then the attacker was gone. She hadn't even had a glimpse of him.

The rain had begun in earnest now. It pattered on the stoop and drummed loudly on the roof of the mobile home. Her caftan was getting wet. Damn, why wouldn't the door open? She jiggled the knob, then pulled the key out. Well, no wonder. She had the wrong key. She found the right one and the door opened easily.

As she entered the dim interior, she stepped over a white piece of paper which had been pushed under her door in her absence. She bent to pick it up, knowing what it was without unfolding it. It looked like the others. She unfolded it anyway and read:

GET OUT OF EAGLE ROCK OR
YOU'LL BE SORRY—
THIS IS YOUR LAST WARNING!!!

Like the two previous anonymous notes she'd received, this one was hand-printed in childlike block letters on plain white paper.

Talia told herself that anonymous threats were more bluster than statements of fact. People who handled their aggressions in that way were too cowardly to act. But after the attack, she'd had a few doubts about that. Obviously it wasn't true, if the person who'd attacked her in the dark was the one sending the notes. But it didn't have to be the same person. Half the residents of Eagle Rock wanted her to leave, and she suspected that two or three of them might resort to beating her to get her out.

Her heart pounded faster and her chest clutched with frustration and, yes, fear. After all, it *was* frightening not to be able to put a face on your enemy. This unfocused fear, which had escalated with each additional threat, had made her jumpy and less open, even with the women who had stuck by her in the rift between her and Agasuyed. It had upset the serenity that was the goal of her inner life and invaded the peaceful home she'd made for herself here, and that filled her with resentment. She thought suddenly of the disapproving Reverend McCall. Why couldn't people just leave other people alone?

Wadding the note angrily, she went to the kitchen and threw it into the basket beneath the sink. In the bed near her front steps, purple petunias and pink impatiens drooped under the rain, which the earth took in hungrily. She loved it here, felt connected to the earth in a way that she'd never experienced before. She owned this acre of land. She *would not* let them scare her into abandoning it and Eagle Rock.

Gripping the edge of the sink, she closed her eyes and practiced breathing slowly and deeply. It helped. Her heartbeat slowed and the knot in her chest relaxed.

Raindrops tapped on the window over the sink and trickled down the glass like tears. The mobile home felt stuffy after being closed up all morning. She cranked open the window a couple of inches and breathed in the pleasant smell of rain.

Then she ran water into the tea kettle and set it on the stove to heat. When the kettle whistled, she made a cup of chamomile tea, taking it into the living room.

She sat on the couch and took a sip, savoring the taste and warmth that soothed and relaxed her throat muscles. Eyes closed, she fixed her mind on her special place of mental healing, her power place, a deep, green, shady glade with a clear stream trickling slowly over a rocky bed. In her mind she walked to the stream and sat down on the soft, grassy, wildflower-strewn bank. She stayed there until she'd finished the tea.

She needed to change out of the damp caftan, but now that she was so relaxed there was something else she wanted to do first. Two decks of cards—the Sacred Pathway Cards and the Medicine Cards—were stacked at one end of the coffee table. She closed her eyes, raised her hand above her head and brought it down at random. When she looked, she saw she'd touched the Sacred Pathway deck. She picked it up and shuffled the cards several times, cut them, and laid the deck facedown on the table. For just an instant, she hesitated.

Taking a deep breath, she turned over the top card. It was the Power Place card, drawing attention to her connection to the Earth Mother and challenging her to find the power place inside her body. She had already done that; she hadn't needed the reminder. But she took a moment to consciously claim the truth that her inner power place would equip her to face all opposition with steadfastness and peace.

The second card was the Rites of Passage. It stood for moving in a different direction, discovering that new paths are available. Talia frowned. Were the cards trying to tell her that she was being obstinate in her refusal to leave Eagle Rock, that she should look for another pathway? She put that possibility aside for the moment and recalled other lessons taught by that particular card. The Rites of Passage card served to remind her that she had earned the right to enter a new level of life, that she was growing, evolving. So perhaps the pathway the card was directing her toward was not a material one, but a state of mind.

The third card depicted a council fire. It taught the necessity of coming to terms with truth, ending confusion by making a decision. Pensively, Talia laid that one down, face up. She was not yet certain what decision the cards were urging her to make.

She picked up the next card, the North Shield, which stood for wisdom and gratitude. True wisdom, according to the sacred path, was found in giving thanks for all the lessons of one's experience, no matter how difficult. It challenged the reader to connect to the Elder within the Self.

It was the fourth card, and four was a sacred number in Cherokee mythology. Talia pressed the card to her breast and closed her eyes. Everything that happened to a person in life contained messages meant to make one wiser. Therefore, the hateful anonymous notes, even the nighttime attack, were teaching her a lesson, although she had not grasped it yet. The Elder within would show her the meaning if she were patient. She gave thanks for the anonymous notes, as the sacred path taught. She could not bring herself to be thankful for the beating.

But eventually, if she remained connected to the power place within, the lesson of the notes and the attack would be revealed to her.

When she opened her eyes, she turned over the fifth card, which was the Drum, signifying Earth Mother's heartbeat, and the sixth, the West Shield, which stood for finding your own answers, going within to listen. The fifth and sixth cards taught lessons it was good to be reminded of. But she was eager to get to the seventh card. Seven was the most sacred number in Cherokee mythology.

She hesitated, taking several deep, calming breaths. Then she turned over the seventh card. It was the Shawl, the card that stood for returning home. There were, of course, many meanings of home in the sacred path—the home of the heart, embracing and loving the true Self, coming back to the natural way of being, being secure in your balance and center.

But to Talia, the lesson the seventh card was teaching was very clear. She had come home to Eagle Rock, and she would overcome all obstacles to stay.

A crack of thunder rocked the mobile home. In Cherokee folk tales, thunder was explained as the noise made by the Thunder Boys wrestling. The Thunder Boys and their father were said to be friendly to Cherokees. To Talia, the thunder sounded like a resounding round of applause. She smiled, more sure than ever that she had read the cards correctly.

She fanned out the seven cards on the coffee table and meditated on the attributes of each one.

A deep calmness descended on her. She imagined a soft blanket of serenity, like cotton batting, wrapping itself around her, protecting her, soothing her. She hugged it close.

She would need it tonight when she summoned Ulenahiha from the spirit world.

The telephone rang, startling her. She knew who it was even before she reached for the phone.

"Hello."

Without identifying himself, he said, "I miss you."

The mere sound of his voice sent a tingle through her. "Me too."

"I have to see you. Can we meet tonight?"

"What time?"

"Nine?"

"Same place?"

"Uh-huh. I'll be waiting for you at the back door."

"I can't wait."

"God, neither can I. I want you."

"Mmmm, me too. I'll be there at nine, and I can stay two or three hours. I do have another appointment at midnight."

"Midnight? Hmmm, that's intriguing."

"It's meant to be."

"You have another date?" He was teasing her, she could hear the smile in his voice.

"Of course." She laughed. "Just so you don't take me for granted."

"I would never do that."

"Good."

"So are you going to tell me what's happening at midnight?"

"I'll tell you everything when we meet."

Listen! Ha! Now you have drawn near to hearken,
O most powerful Red Raven.

6

Gentle rain fell, off and on, all evening and into the night, soaking the earth, blessing it.

A few minutes after midnight, Talia Wind parked at the Native American Research Library in a drive circling from the highway, on the west side of the building, along the front, which faced south, and back around to the highway again. She parked next to a row of tall shrubs which screened the car from the view of anyone traveling the highway.

She turned off the motor. For a few moments, she stayed in the car, near the bottom of the library steps, looking around her and listening to the silence.

The building was a black hulk surrounded by shadows. Except for a pool of light from a pole lamp in front of the library, there were no streetlights this far out of town. A single pale yellow rectangle marked one window of the library, where a light had been left on inside, behind closed blinds.

The only other light in the vicinity came from Dowell's foreign car dealership a good distance north of the library. Dowell's light backlit the wooden gallows to the east of the library. The gallows was as exact a replica of the original as it had been possible to construct from the few remaining sketches.

Talia got out of her car, glancing at the gallows, which loomed menacingly, as she approached the library. She wondered why the foundation had felt it necessary to restore *that* as well as the building. She also wondered how many people had died there—not on that gallows, but on the original one which had been in the same place.

Had one of them been Ulenahiha?

A shiver ran up her spine.

She shook it off and lifted her face to the night sky. The rain had stopped, but the air remained heavy with humidity, as if the air itself was made up of tiny, floating particles of water.

She smiled as she recalled the happiness of the last three hours. She could still smell him, still feel his hands on her body. She loved being with him, but hated having to steal the time like a thief. She wanted to be with him openly and all the time. Tonight he had said he'd find a way for them to be together always, somehow.

She climbed the steps to the front door. With the aid of her flashlight, she let herself in with the key Ridge had given her. In addition to the flashlight, she'd brought a bag containing the things she would need for the medicine ceremony.

A single low-wattage bulb had been left on in the reference room, bathing the foyer in a faint, otherworldly glow. Flicking off her flashlight, Talia paused just inside the door to absorb the library's atmosphere.

The reference room, with the glass door where a library employee had seen the ghost's reflection, was on her right. Gradually, she was able to see the computer on the desk to her left. Behind the desk and straight ahead of her, barred doors led into other rooms. In restoring and transforming the building, the foundation had left as much of the original jail as possible, like the heavy steel-barred doors—now painted white—behind which prisoners of the Cherokee Nation had once been caged. Now the barred doors stood open and the cells were lined with books.

The stillness was mesmerizing, and Talia felt herself being lulled by it. Then a soft, scurrying sound made her heart leap in her chest. She peered at the black hole where stairs descended to the basement. The sound had come from down there.

A mouse, she told herself. Since returning to her Cherokee roots, she had come to believe that every animal has a spirit and must be respected—even a mouse. But if ignored and given enough time, mice would destroy a library. She must remember to tell Ridge to catch it in a trap and set it free in the woods.

She turned her mind to Ulenahiha.

I come as a friend. I come to release you.

She walked slowly through the library, touching things, pausing every few steps to look and listen. She felt no sense of the ghost's presence.

She glanced at the stairwell again. Except for the reflection in the glass door and the change of the file name in the computer, all the manifestations had been audible ones and had occurred in the basement. Again, she reached into her bag for the flashlight and turned it on. Following the beam, she walked back across the small foyer to the wide staircase and descended.

The basement was a single room with a concrete floor and the original walls, made of huge, hand-hewn stones, exposed. A long wood table stood in the center of the room with molded green plastic chairs around it. Cabinets, a small sink, a range top with a copper hood, and a microwave oven lined one wall. A copy machine sat against the opposite wall. In one corner, card tables held stacks of paper, brochures, bookmarks, and a few books in need of rebinding.

Running her fingers around beneath the range hood, Talia found the light switch, flipped on the soft hood light, and turned off the flashlight. She would need a little light, but not so much that it would disturb the atmosphere.

Before the attack at Eagle Rock, she had never been afraid of the dark, even as a child. She liked being alone at night, had always thought of darkness as her friend. In the silent dark, distractions were diminished. In the stillness she could let her mind go inside to her power place or roam outward, free of restraints. She would not let what had happened at Eagle Rock change that. But tonight she wanted enough light to see a visible manifestation, should there be one.

After laying the flashlight and her bag on the table, she walked slowly around the room, opening her mind to whatever impressions might be present. She sensed nothing. The ghost was in hiding. He might not come out at all tonight. Even if he did, it could take until dawn to coax him into revealing himself.

In that case, she'd better get started.

After careful consideration, she had left the cards and her crystals at home. She brought from her bag a small pouch of tobacco and a pipe, tobacco being the favored means of Cherokee priests in ancient times for making contact with the spirit world. She sat down, took out the pipe and tobacco pouch, and laid them on the table.

Talia did not smoke. She abhorred the thought of putting any harmful substance into her body, and she had at first resisted using tobacco.

About a month after she arrived at Eagle Rock, she had gone into the woods on a vision quest. She had stayed in the woods for three days and nights without food or water before she was given her vision, in which it was revealed to her that, while the habitual use of tobacco was harmful, its sacramental use was a gift from the Earth Mother.

Thereafter, she had eagerly recorded whatever medicine ceremonies Agasuyed was willing to teach her—before Agasuyed decided she was encroaching on his territory and cut off the lessons. By then, Talia had discovered other sources such as manuscripts and books and no longer needed Agasuyed. Now, she used tobacco when the occasion seemed to call for it, but she didn't inhale.

She had continued the Cherokee language courses, too, but it was clear that she had no gift for languages. She had copied the incantations for various medicine ceremonies on cards in Cherokee, with the pronunciation carefully printed beneath the Cherokee syllables in English letters, to ensure she would make no mistakes. A single mistake could nullify the incantation.

Now she took from her bag a cigarette lighter and the card containing the incantation she would use to remake the tobacco, infuse it with magic power, and summon the ghost. She put the lighter aside for the moment and laid the card at the edge of the table, where the light from the range hood fell on it. She opened the pouch.

Carefully, she poured the tobacco into her cupped palm and held it up in front of her. She began chanting the incantation slowly and softly, in Cherokee.

Listen! Ha! You have strayed from the pathway.
Now you have drawn near to hearken.
You are resting directly overhead.
O Black Raven, you never fail in anything.
Ha! Now you are brought down.
Ha! There shall be left no more than a trace upon the ground where you have been.
You have now put it into a crevice in a high mountain, that it may never find the way back.
You have put it to rest in the Darkening Land, so that it may never return.
Let relief come.
Listen! Ha! Now you have drawn near to hearken.
O most powerful Red Raven.
Ha! You never fail in anything, for so it was ordained of you.
Ha! You are resting . . .

When she finished the incantation, an extraordinarily long one, she began again, feeling the lulling, hypnotic power of the chanting. She was aware of the silence around her as she chanted the words. If the ghost was there, he was listening and waiting.

Four repetitions were usually enough to remake the tobacco before it was ready for smoking, but sometimes seven were required.

She would sense when it was time to stop.

She began the third repetition.

Listen! Ha! . . .

Outside the library, all was quiet. Few cars passed along the highway at that time of night.

The shrubs surrounding the library were humped, black shadows, hugging the foundation as if for protection from the night.

Stealthily, a moving shadow approached the shrubbery, separated the branches in a particular place in the wall, and halted abruptly. Low, droning sounds came from inside the library. Someone was talking, but the words were indistinguishable.

After a few moments of hesitation, the shadow backed away quietly, letting the branches drop back into place.

Talia was outside in a place she could not identify. The only light came from a quarter-moon. To her right, a shadow moved from behind a tree and came toward her. Dimly, the shadow took the shape of a man, dragging chains from his wrists and ankles. As he came closer, she saw that the figure's head was a skull with gaping black eyeholes.

Terror gripped her. She tried to cry out, to call for help, but the only sound she was capable of uttering was a pitiful whimper. She tried to run and found that she couldn't move. Her heartbeat thundered in her ears.

She was going to die . . .

*   *   *

Talia jerked awake. She had been somewhere else, struggling in dark dreams that still dragged at her like a treacherous undertow. She shook off the weight of sleep and forced her eyes open. The frightening current of dreams ebbed and faded away.

Her face was damp with perspiration. She used the hem of her full skirt to wipe it dry.

After completing the medicine ceremony, she had remained seated, waiting, fighting the need of her eyelids to droop. Finally, unable to stay awake any longer, she had drifted into sleep, her head resting on her crossed arms on the table. Now she felt stiff and sore. Darkness still pressed against the high windows along one side of the half-basement. How long had she slept?

She stood to peer at the range clock. It read two-fourteen. She had slept for over an hour. She glanced around, her gaze probing the dark corners of the basement, scanning the blank wall opposite the windows. On that side of the building, the ground dipped sharply, leaving the entire wall above ground.

Had the ghost come and gone?

She couldn't do another medicine ceremony because all the tobacco she'd brought with her had been reduced to ashes. Maybe she should have brought her crystals, after all. Or perhaps patience was all she needed.

She would stay until the first hint of dawn touched the basement windows, she decided. If Ulenahiha did not make himself known, she would leave and return to try again tomorrow night. Next time she would bring her crystals and her cards, along with the pipe and more tobacco.

She was disappointed in herself for falling asleep. If she

had to come back tomorrow, she'd take a nap in the afternoon so it wouldn't happen again.

But there was still time tonight . . .

Closing her eyes, she imagined her mind opening, like a rosebud, petal by petal, until all barriers fell, leaving the pathway clear for a message from the spirit world.

When the sound came, she was not, after all, ready for it. She jerked so violently she came half out of her chair. She heard heavy chains being dragged across the ground, as if a chained prisoner was being led to the gallows.

Deana Cloud had heard the same sound the night she worked alone in the library, and Talia had heard it in her dream. She recalled the figure in the shadows, the chains dragging from his wrists and ankles. She must have heard the sound in her sleep and it had become a part of the dream. Or vision. Sometimes Talia could not distinguish between the two. She thought of dreams and visions as merely other dimensions of reality which she visited occasionally.

Now, in the library basement, in the dimension called "real life" by people who recognized no other, silence had returned.

Grabbing her flashlight, she flicked it on, sending the beam in a full circle around the basement. Everything was as it had been before. Perhaps she had not been meant to return to real life when she did. Perhaps the ghost had entered her dream and had been about to communicate with her when she awoke. Did the chains mean that he had, indeed, been a prisoner in this jail when he was alive? Had he died on the gallows a few feet from where she stood?

Suddenly the sound of dragging chains came again, briefly, and then the silence returned.

She glanced at the open doorway which led to the stairs. The sound had seemed to come from above her. The ghost was upstairs.

She walked to the door, paused to let her heartbeat slow, then shone her light on the stairs. She was trembling and the beam moved erratically. She pressed her arm against her side to stop the shaking. With an effort, she stifled a feeling that something wasn't right. She had summoned the ghost and he had come. Why was she afraid?

She paused on each step to listen. But she heard nothing more.

When she reached the foyer, she played the flashlight beam over the desks and into the book-lined cell rooms surrounding the foyer. Finally, she went into the reference room. She saw nothing unusual, nothing out of place.

She switched off the flashlight and stood in the eerie dimness, listening, waiting, willing the sound to come again so that she could pinpoint where it came from.

Ulenahiha was here. She could feel him. But he remained silent. Was he testing her to see if she was strong enough to overcome her fear and face him?

She thought back to her dream, tried to re-create it with all the details. In the dream she had been out-of-doors, but she didn't know exactly where, although that didn't mean the setting was unknown to her. It was possible the darkness had obscured familiar landmarks she might otherwise have recognized.

She had seen a shadowy figure, a man in chains. The figure had come toward her slowly, but after she saw that his face was a fleshless skull, she'd awakened. Yet she'd heard the chains again, twice, after she was awake.

In the dream, Ulenahiha may have tried to tell her that he would not communicate with her inside the library. Maybe he wanted her to go outside.

But where?

The fact that the ghost was in chains could mean that he was headed for the gallows. Was that where Ulenahiha wanted to contact her? It felt right.

All she had was the dream and her instincts. She would follow them.

She returned to the foyer, opened the door, and stepped out on a concrete landing with wide steps leading down to the ground. She still held the flashlight, started to turn it on, but changed her mind because, in the dream, she'd had no light. She would continue to let her instincts guide her.

She descended the steps quietly and paused at the bottom of the stairs to listen, but she heard nothing. Gripping the flashlight tightly in one hand, she turned to her left and walked across thick grass, around to the east side of the library.

The dark shadow of a tree trunk materialized near the back corner of the library. She hadn't come around to this side of the building when she arrived, so she hadn't seen the tree. Yet it looked familiar somehow. Was it the tree in her dream, where the ghost had been standing when she first saw him?

She walked closer to the gallows. Her heightened senses picked up the soft tread of footfalls. She halted uncertainly, straining to hear. Nothing. She looked around but saw no ghostlike figure.

The footsteps had stopped, if she'd really heard them in the first place. She was so tense that she could have imagined them. The only sound now was the sound of her own breathing.

She closed her eyes, willing herself to relax. "I come as a friend," she whispered. "I come to release you, Ulenahiha."

She heard nothing. She squinted into the darkness, searching for Ulenahiha.

The black hulk of the gallows rose before her, one of its heavy wood posts blotting out the moon.

Then she heard the footsteps again, growing dimmer, moving away from her. She followed the sound.

Ha! You never fail in anything,
for so it was ordained of you.

7

Monday morning, Ridge Wind arrived at the library early, more than an hour before the library opened at eight, the time that ordinarily marked the start of his workday. He'd been awake since five, vaguely anxious and unable to sleep. Finally, he had given up trying, had decided to come to the library, make coffee, maybe run out for doughnuts before Alice and Deana got there.

His aunt Talia had promised to call him when she left the library, no matter what time it was. He didn't care if she woke him up, he'd insisted. He wanted to know what had happened, if she'd made contact with Ulenahiha. But she hadn't called, and when he'd finally given in to his curiosity and phoned her at six-thirty that morning, he'd gotten the answering machine, which she used to screen her calls, to avoid talking to her ex-husband. Ridge had identified himself and gave her plenty of time to pick up. But she didn't. She must have fallen into an exhausted sleep after returning home from the library, a sleep so deep that the phone hadn't awakened her.

It was a reasonable explanation, but still he couldn't shake a feeling of unease. He wouldn't be rid of the feeling until he talked to Talia. Not that he believed Ulenahiha would harm her. The ghost had never shown an inclination to hurt anyone. Ulenahiha was a benign ghost, more to be pitied than feared.

It was just that Ridge couldn't figure out why Talia hadn't called. Talia didn't break promises.

He parked behind the library beside an old Honda Civic, recognizing it as the one Molly Bearpaw had been driving yesterday at the church. Must have given her some trouble on the way home and she'd pulled off the road and left it. A few hundred yards more, and she could have abandoned it at Dowell's. Evidently she couldn't coax it that far.

He fingered the keys on his chain, picking out the one that unlocked the library's back door. He'd loaned his front door key to Talia. He let himself in and flipped on the lights. A quick glance told him that everything was as he'd left it Saturday at noon. There was no evidence that Talia or anyone else had been there, except for a faint scent of tobacco in the air.

He clambered down the stairs and flipped on the basement light as he entered the room. An old-fashioned clay pipe with a few ashes left in the bowl, a cigarette lighter, a small cotton pouch with a string tie, and an index card with writing on it lay on the table. Ridge picked up the pouch and sniffed the scent of the tobacco it had held. A canvas bag sat on the floor beneath the table. He picked it up and looked inside. It was empty except for a ring of keys. These were Talia's things. Why had she left them behind?

Remembering Deana's reaction to hearing the ghost when she was alone in the library, he wondered if Ulenahiha could have frightened Talia into fleeing the building without her belongings. But that didn't seem likely. Talia had come there to communicate with the ghost. Why would she run away when she succeeded?

Puzzling over these things, Ridge dropped the pipe, lighter, tobacco pouch, and index card into the canvas bag and set it on the table. He gazed around the familiar room, uncertain what to do next. He'd make coffee and try calling Talia again in a few minutes.

He rinsed out the glass pot, added a paper filter to the automatic drip coffeemaker, spooned in coffee grounds, and pressed the "on" switch.

While the coffee brewed, he went back upstairs and dialed Talia's number, and again he got the answering machine. He left a message for her to call him at the library.

The smell of fresh-made coffee drifted up from the basement. It was five minutes before seven, and the best doughnut shop in town opened at seven. He'd get a half-dozen glazed and a couple of the cinnamon rolls that Alice loved. Then he could drive out to Eagle Rock and check on Talia and still be back before Alice and Deana came to work.

He went to the front window in the foyer and opened the slatted blind. The morning was clear, the sun sucking up the remains of humidity from the night before.

A white car was parked in front of the library. He hadn't noticed it before because tall shrubs blocked the view in front of the library from the road, and he'd entered by the back door. He tugged on the cord that lifted the blind, raising it to the top of the window.

He stared at the white Ford. He couldn't see anyone inside, but the car looked like Talia's. He remained frozen at the window for a long moment, trying to make sense of it. Then he ran back downstairs and pulled the keys from the bag. One of them was Talia's car key.

Ridge groped for an explanation. Maybe the Ford, like Molly Bearpaw's Civic, wouldn't start when Talia was ready to leave, so she'd called someone to pick her up. But if Talia had needed a ride, she knew he was waiting to hear from her. Wouldn't she have called him?

Where was she?

Something was very wrong.

Heart pounding, he ran back upstairs and started toward the front door before he remembered that he didn't have his key and couldn't disengage the bolt without it. The front door key was still in Talia's bag. Instead of going downstairs again, he turned around and hurried to the back door and let himself out.

He clambered down the three steps and turned left to go around to the front of the library. Then he caught a movement to his right from the corner of his eye. Every muscle in his body tensed and his head jerked around, letting him know how deeply anxious he was. Talia's leaving her medicine paraphernalia behind and not answering her phone—he could manage to explain all that to himself. But she wouldn't leave her car.

Cool it, man, he told himself, as he walked toward the east side of the library where he'd seen the faint movement. At first, he could see, at the corner of the building, what looked like a piece of cloth fluttering in the breeze—the movement that had caught his eye. As he drew nearer the corner, part of the gallows came into view, and he could see more of the fluttering cloth. It looked like a woman's skirt. As that thought registered, he walked close enough to see a few inches of slender leg and a foot encased in a brown leather shoe.

The truth exploded in his brain.

Something was hanging from the gallows. *Something.* He wouldn't let himself think someone.

He started to run. It's a dummy, he told himself, remembering the one kids had strung up on the gallows last Halloween. It's just somebody's sick idea of a joke. He leaped over a flashlight lying on the ground as he crossed the graveled area surrounding the gallows, and halted, his breath coming in labored gasps.

It wasn't a dummy. It was a woman, her head dropped forward, long dark hair obscuring her face.

Who . . . ? Still, his mind balked at the logical answer. It couldn't be. Could not be!

Heart pumping furiously, he scrambled up the steps to the gallows and grabbed the body around the legs, lifting it. Now he could see the rope around her neck, and as he stood there, holding the weight of the body, the long hair swung to one side, exposing her face, and he could no longer deny what a part of his mind had known all along.

It was Talia, her face a ghastly blue-gray color, eyes bulging, her tongue swollen, lolling, her mouth set in a rictus of terror. She was barely recognizable. He knew that he was far too late to save her, but he couldn't leave her hanging there like that.

Cursing, he tried to free her from the noose. But he couldn't. He would have to climb up and cut her down. Without warning, a sob ripped through his chest, and tears blurred his vision as he released the body and got out his pocketknife.

Only later did it occur to him that he was tampering with evidence. All he could think of in that moment was that he had to get her down. Grabbing hold of Talia's shoulders with one arm, he reached up and sliced through the rope with his knife.

As gently as possible, he laid her on the wood gallows floor and pulled her skirt down to cover her thighs, which were mottled a hideous purple blue color.

Then he ran to the back door of the library. He rushed to the nearest telephone, looked at the list of emergency numbers on a sticker attached to the base, and fixed on the word "Police." He dialed.

"I found my aunt," he blurted when a dispatcher answered. "She was on the gallows—she's dead!"

"Okay, now. Slow down, mister. Did you say gallows?"

"The gallows—at the library."

"What library?"

How many libraries had a gallows, for God's sake? Ridge felt his grip on himself slipping. "The Native American Research Library, dammit!"

"Look, mister, I told you to calm down, okay? I know where you are now. That's outside the city limits in the County Sheriff's jurisdiction."

He knew that, of course, but he wasn't thinking exactly straight. Ridge slammed the phone down and found the number of the Sheriff's office.

The full reality of what had happened was finally sinking in. Had Talia committed suicide? Yesterday at the wild onion breakfast, she'd seemed the same as she usually did, certainly not depressed or excessively worried. The preacher had gotten her back up a little, but she wouldn't kill herself over that. It made no sense at all.

His hand shook violently as he dialed.

"Why did you cut her down if you could see she was already dead?" demanded Sheriff Claude Hobart—for at least the fourth time.

Ridge Wind sat behind the desk in the library foyer, his head in his hands. His sister, Natalie, sat on the desktop, next to the computer, her head bowed, her blue-jeaned legs dangling. Ridge had caught her in her dorm room before she left for breakfast. She'd arrived in time to see Talia's body. Ridge had had to pull her away, take her into the library and get her calmed down. Now she was quiet, but every few minutes fresh rivulets of tears trickled down her face.

Deana Cloud and Alice Mundy, who'd arrived ten minutes ago, sat in two chairs against the wall. Both seemed stunned into muteness. Deana kept wiping her eyes and blowing her nose. Alice, a trim, fortyish Cherokee woman, appeared even more dazed than Deana, as though she simply couldn't comprehend what had happened.

The Sheriff paced back and forth across the foyer, firing questions, mostly at Ridge, since the women hadn't been there when the body was discovered.

Molly was observing all this from where she stood, leaning against a wall of books, taking notes as Ridge answered Hobart's questions. She had been informed of Talia Wind's death by D.J., who'd taken Ridge's call to the Sheriff's office less than an hour before his night shift ended. He'd picked up Molly on his way to the scene, arriving a few minutes ahead of Deana and Alice, just as an ambulance was driving away with the body. D.J. and another Sheriff's deputy were still combing the area around the gallows for evidence.

"I just wanted to get her down," Ridge said wearily, for the fourth time. "I couldn't stand seeing her like that." He'd rubbed his eyes with his fists until angry red streaked the white around his dark pupils. His handsome face was drawn, as if a hand had gripped his chin and pulled down so hard it had stretched his face, making the high cheekbones and square jaw more prominent, the bones pushing against the skin.

"But you said you could tell she was already dead," said Hobart doggedly, "and still you cut her down."

Ridge drew a shaky breath. "I wasn't thinking."

The Sheriff, a stocky man in his sixties and nearing retirement, glared at Ridge suspiciously, as though he thought cutting down Talia's body had been part of a plan to conceal evidence. Hobart hated having people die in his jurisdiction under suspicious circumstances because it made extra work for the Sheriff's Department. Hobart wanted to slide through his last couple of years as Sheriff on a rippleless stream of status quo. Having to investigate a death irritated him, and he tended to snap at people. He particularly disliked investigating a death when the Cherokee police were involved. He considered their new Major Crimes Unit an affront to his ability to do his job without outside help.

"So the victim came here in the middle of the night for some kind of—er, exorcism?"

"Something like that, yes," Ridge replied. "Actually, it was a medicine ceremony. You saw her pipe and tobacco pouch downstairs." He had briefly summarized Talia's reason for being in the library at night, substituting "unhealthy atmosphere" for "ghost." Molly guessed that Ridge thought the Sheriff would scoff or accuse him of lying if he said the library was haunted.

"And you say it was about seven when you found her?" Hobart asked.

"A few minutes before seven," Ridge said shortly, irritated at being asked to repeat himself again.

"But the library doesn't open till eight."

Ridge lifted his head and confronted the Sheriff's gaze. "I was worried because Aunt Talia hadn't called me, like she promised, and she wasn't answering her phone. I couldn't sleep, so I came down early. Is that a crime?"

"Don't get smart with me, mister."

"I'm sorry, but you keep asking these questions I've already answered."

"They'll do an autopsy, you know," Hobart said darkly. "The Medical Examiner can tell exactly how long she's been dead."

Molly watched the Sheriff watching Ridge Wind. Hobart made it sound as though Doc Pohl could pinpoint the very minute when Talia drew her last breath, which was nonsense.

Ridge shrugged wearily. "That won't tell you who killed her, though, will it?"

"You keep saying somebody killed her. How do you know she didn't kill herself?"

Natalie twisted around to glare at the Sheriff. Her eyes were puffy from crying. "You didn't know Aunt Talia. She would never have killed herself."

Hobart gazed at her thoughtfully. "So tell me who might've had it in for her."

Ridge and Natalie exchanged a long look. Finally, Ridge said, "She and her ex-husband weren't on very good terms, but I can't believe he'd kill her."

Hobart pulled a stubby pencil and what looked like a gas station receipt from his shirt pocket. A strand of white hair fell forward to rake his eyebrows as he turned the receipt over to the blank side and snapped, "What's his name?"

"Dell Greer," Ridge said. "He lives out at Eagle Rock."

"Didn't you say that's where your aunt lived?"

Ridge nodded. "They were married when they moved there. They got a divorce a few months back and both of them stayed on."

"Anybody else you can think of who might have wanted to harm your aunt?"

When Ridge didn't respond immediately, Natalie cleared her throat and said firmly, "Agasuyed Beaver."

Hobart gave her a long, penetrating look. "The guy who used to own all that Eagle Rock land? Some kind of medicine man, isn't he?"

Natalie nodded. "Aunt Talia organized meditation groups and vision quests for the women. Agasuyed didn't like it. He didn't want anybody else, especially a woman, stealing any of his thunder."

Hobart looked over at Molly and rolled his eyes, as if to say, This is your territory. *You* deal with it.

"Talia had received some anonymous notes, telling her to leave Eagle Rock," Molly put in.

Hobart whirled around. "And you think it was this Agasuyed who sent the notes?"

Molly shrugged. "I wouldn't know about that."

"Well, I would," Natalie flared. "Of course Agasuyed sent

those notes! He tried to buy Aunt Talia's land, but she re-fused, so he sent Dell Greer to make an offer. Dell's his little stooge. Agasuyed's tried every trick in the book to force Aunt Talia to move."

Hobart's expression was doubtful. "I'll have a talk with him. Greer, too."

Deana made a little whimpering sound. The others turned to look at her in astonishment. She'd hardly said three words since she arrived. "It wasn't him," she blurted, her voice high and shrill. "Everybody else is afraid to say it, so I will. *He* did it!" she said, and her voice broke.

"You talking about the medicine man?" Hobart asked.

She shook her head vigorously. "No. Ulenahiha killed her."

The Sheriff looked bewildered. Alice finally spoke. "Ulenahiha is the ghost who lives in the library. Talia was trying to release him so he could go to the Nightland."

"Oh, for the—" Hobart sputtered to a stop, tilting his head to look at the ceiling. He wiped his palm down over his face and composed himself. "I'm finished here for now. Might have to come back after I hear from the Medical Examiner. But I doubt it." He glanced at Alice and shook his head. "And don't feed me any more of that ghost stuff." He clomped out.

Molly followed and caught up with him on the library steps. "Are you going out to Eagle Rock now, Sheriff?"

He turned around, raking her with a disgruntled look. "Thought I might. Somebody ought to tell the Beavers and the woman's ex-husband what's happened."

"Mind if I come along? I'm without transportation at the moment."

He hesitated, sighed, then gestured with one hand. "I'll get one of the deputies to take you," he said stiffly. He had to co-operate with Cherokee Nation law enforcement people—or get heavy flak from the large Cherokee population of the county—but he didn't have to like it. He circled around the library. "You men about finished here?"

"Yeah," D.J. said. He came toward them, carrying a flash-light in a plastic sack. The other deputy was Stanley Brock, who was young and green—he'd only been a deputy a few weeks. He and D.J. were sharing the night shift this month so that D.J. could oversee Brock's on-the-job training.

"We couldn't pick up any definite footprints near the gal-lows," D.J. said. "The ground around it is covered with gravel, and beyond that it's all grass. You can see some impressions of what could be footprints, but not enough to tell what kind of shoes made them or even what size. Nothing very helpful in her car, either. We *were* able to lift a few clear prints there. I left the keys in the ignition."

Hobart nodded. "The prints will probably all turn out to be the victim's. The woman killed herself." He paused, think-ing. "I want you to follow me out to Eagle Rock, Kennedy. Take Molly with you. Brock, you can go on home." The Sher-iff turned and walked toward his car. "Oh," he said, turning back. "Kennedy, get that canvas bag we saw in the basement. It belonged to Talia Wind. That's where I found her car keys. We better hang on to it till we get the ME's report."

Molly wanted another look at the basement, anyway. She'd only had a glimpse of it when she arrived and found the Sher-iff down there. But he'd returned to the upper level when Molly joined him.

She followed D.J. toward the library. He paused on the steps. "How are the niece and nephew taking it?"

"They're stunned, grieving, about what you'd expect. And they both insist Talia didn't kill herself. They think either her ex-husband or Agasuyed Beaver murdered her."

He lifted his brows. "Could be just denial. Family members have a hard time with suicide sometimes."

As if Molly didn't know that from personal experience. "Maybe, but I talked to Talia Wind yesterday at church. She didn't strike me as suicidal, either."

D.J. studied her face for an instant, then shook his head. They entered the library.

Ridge and Natalie were sitting where the Sheriff had left them. Deana and Alice were milling around, as though unsure what to do next. Natalie tried to work up a smile for D.J., but it was clearly an effort.

Molly put her arm around the girl. "Are you okay?"

"Yeah," she sighed. "We have to call our folks and I dread that. Dad and Talia were pretty close. They'll want to drive up from Idabel today, so I may not be able to make it to the office this afternoon."

"Of course you won't. Don't even try."

"We'll have to take those things your aunt left in the basement," D.J. said to Ridge. "It's evidence. We may be able to get them back to you as soon as we get the Medical Examiner's report. Depends."

It depended on whether Pohl thought the death was a suicide or foul play, Molly thought.

Ridge nodded numbly. "Go ahead."

D.J. descended the basement stairs, Molly at his heels.

The canvas bag containing Talia Wind's pipe, tobacco pouch, lighter, and an index card with a Cherokee incantation printed on it sat on the conference table. Molly had looked inside when she'd come down earlier.

Talia had evidently conducted the medicine ceremony in the basement. Molly walked around the room, taking it in, looking for anything that might provide a clue to Talia's death.

D.J. grabbed the bag. "You ready?"

"Give me a minute, okay?"

The only windows in the basement were in the east wall, high up. Did Talia look up, see something outside, and go out to investigate? That could be what happened, Molly thought, since the only thing found outside with the body was a flashlight.

What had drawn Talia outside?

Molly turned away from the windows, scanned the spare furnishings. She took note of the copier and a couple of card tables with papers stacked on top, nothing that shouldn't be there.

The west wall was blank, the original hand-hewn stones exposed. She walked over and ran her hand across the rough sandstone. Grit scraped beneath her shoes, and she looked down. Fine grains of the old mortar had sifted loose and fallen on the floor. Several of the area's early buildings had been constructed of these stones. They were big, two or three feet long by two feet in width, and at least a foot thick. It would take a strong man to have lifted them into place, maybe two as the wall rose higher.

The memory of Rayburn Dowell's words made her smile ruefully.

He went through the wall.

She had wondered if the elder Dowell had actually seen a

man breaking into the library at night. But the windows on the east wall were double-paned and securely locked. The north and south walls were partially underground and had no windows. That left the west wall, the only one that was fully aboveground. Anyone entering that way would have to go through a foot of solid rock. Rayburn Dowell had been hallucinating.

"Come on, Molly," D.J. said impatiently. "Claude will kick my butt if I don't get out to Eagle Rock pretty quick."

"Okay." There was nothing helpful in the basement, after all. Molly followed him up the stairs.

D.J. hesitated in the foyer. "We're finished with your aunt's car," he told Ridge and Natalie. "The keys are still in the ignition."

"Thanks," Ridge murmured.

"Dad will know what to do with the car," Natalie said. She looked at Molly. "I'll try to come to the office tomorrow."

"Don't do that, Nat. I can get along without you for a few days. You'll have family things to do."

She rubbed her swollen eyes. "Molly, I think the Sheriff's going to call this a suicide and close the case."

"All the evidence isn't in yet," Molly said.

"Believe me," Natalie insisted, "she didn't kill herself."

Molly nodded, but she would wait for the Medical Examiner's report before making her own decision.

"You saw her Sunday," Natalie continued. "She acted just like always. How could she do that if she was thinking of killing herself?"

Molly smoothed a hand over Natalie's hair. "Let's wait and see what develops in the next day or two."

Natalie shook her head. "It's going to be up to us to catch her killer."

Molly caught the "us" but chose not to comment on it. Time enough to argue the point after she learned whether she had to get involved in a murder investigation.

"Remember, Nat," Molly said as she left, "you really don't need to come to the office for a few days."

Ha! You are resting directly overhead.
Ha! Now you are brought down.

8

As they drove away from the library, Molly saw Tim Dowell's black Lexus approaching. The car slowed and the driver's tinted window was lowered, exposing Dowell's face. Tim stared curiously at the Sheriff's car as they passed. Molly turned around in her seat and waved. Tim would find out soon enough what had happened at the library. It would be all over town by noon.

"I guess he got his dad settled down all right," D.J. commented.

"Who, Tim Dowell?"

"Yeah. His old man's got Alzheimer's."

"I know. What do you mean about settling him down?"

"Rayburn Dowell took off sometime last night. Tim woke up about five and couldn't find him. They live in Rambling Oaks, outside the city limits, so we caught the call." Rambling Oaks was an upscale addition of homes on half-acre lots.

"Tim looked around the neighborhood, then called us. He was pretty shook up. I gathered it wasn't the first time his dad disappeared, but he always found him nearby."

"But you found him?"

"Yeah, in Town Branch Park, stretched out on one of the picnic tables. I guess he couldn't find his way home, so he just went to sleep."

"Poor man," Molly murmured. "Poor Tim."

D.J. mumbled an assent.

She turned sideways in her seat. "You look beat."

D.J.'s uniform looked as if he'd slept in it for a week and his brown hair was rumpled. D.J. always seemed to look rumpled, like a hyperactive little boy, which Molly found weirdly endearing. But there was nothing endearing about the way he looked now. His brown eyes were weary and the creases on either side of his mouth seemed to have deepened since Molly had last seen him yesterday morning.

"Working nights always gets to me," he said. He reached out to pat her knee, a gesture of reassurance. "I can't sleep well in the daytime. It's unnatural. I'll catch up when I go back on day shift. Did I tell you the Chief Investigator's job will be open next fall? I'm going to apply for it."

"Nick's retiring?"

He nodded.

"Well, you should get the job," Molly said. D.J. had been with the Sheriff's Department for several years and had an exemplary record. The Chief Investigator's job paid a little more than the other deputies earned. Probably more important to D.J., the man who held it worked the day shift all the time.

Molly reached over and put her hand on the back of his neck, kneading the tight muscles.

He sighed gratefully and rolled his head around. "Umm, that feels good."

"I don't know why the Sheriff wanted you to go out to Eagle Rock. Your shift ended at eight."

He grinned. "I'll give you three guesses, Ms. Major Crimes Investigator."

"Me? You mean he doesn't even want me riding in his car?"

"That's my guess. Not only are you an employee of the Cherokee Nation who's going to be looking over his shoulder on this one. You're a woman."

"Well, tough," she muttered and leaned her head against the curve of his shoulder. "The Sheriff needs to get with the times."

D.J. chuckled. He lifted her hand and kissed the knuckles, then wrapped his fingers around hers. "I doubt he's going to change much at this late date."

Molly thought D.J. was right, but she had practice at working around Hobart. "How's Stanley Brock doing?"

"Like an overeager pup. Asks a million dumb questions, but he'll be okay, once he gets the hang of things. I'm glad the Sheriff sent him home. He had a big night."

"Mr. Dowell's disappearance and then Talia, you mean?"

He nodded. "Mostly. But first we had a house burglary north of town. The owners came home to find the house ransacked. Nothing missing, though, except the TV and a shotgun."

"Just what we need, another gun on the street."

"Tell me about it. As soon as we got back to the station from that call, we had a call out east, another car theft. Then we had to round up Rayburn Dowell, and thank goodness he was okay. To cap the night off in a big way, this woman hangs herself."

"Or somebody else does it for her," Molly muttered.

He glanced over at her. "Right, if her niece and nephew are to be believed. Anyway, seeing a dead body on top of the other things really had Brock pumped. I'll be surprised if he can sleep at all, but at least he won't be in the way, asking a million questions."

"Whose car was stolen this time?"

"Old Dr. Ridley's Lincoln." Dr. Ridley had closed his office and stopped seeing patients only a couple of years ago, even though he was pushing eighty.

"Dr. Ridley loves that car," Molly said, "and he's hardly had time to break it in." It was a Lincoln Town Car, white with red leather interior.

"Yeah, he actually cried when Brock and I talked to him. Said he got up to go to the bathroom and looked out the window at the driveway, expecting to see his pride and joy. The Lincoln was gone, and he never heard a thing. Brock and I combed all the roads out east and then we looked all over town, but we didn't see the Lincoln."

"It's getting to be a weekly ritual around here," Molly muttered.

"Stolen cars? I happened to look over our records for the past two years. The number of cars stolen in the county *has* gone up in the past six months, by ten or fifteen percent. Not as much as I thought, though."

"That's hard to believe. Lately, I hear people around town talking about it all the time."

"Some of the recent victims have been prominent citizens,

so I guess that's why people are more aware of the problem. Plus this thief seems to only take new, expensive cars."

"Do you have any leads at all?"

"Very few. But I think it's a professional, somebody from out of town. Has to be. I don't think we have anybody that slick around here. He's in the car and on the road in a minute or less. Probably drives straight to a chop shop and by morning the car is nothing but spare parts."

"That beautiful Lincoln," Molly mourned, imagining its various parts stacked like cordwood.

"We need an extra deputy on the night shift, just to patrol for potential car thieves. But there's no money in the budget for another man. We just got the funds to give the deputies a five percent raise, first raise we've had in four years."

"No wonder the Sheriff is in such a grouchy mood. He can't catch the car thief and now he's got a dead body on his hands and Talia's niece and nephew insist it wasn't suicide."

"It *is* an odd place to do it. Why would she drive to the library from Eagle Rock to do a medicine ceremony and suddenly decide to hang herself?"

"Besides which, Talia Wind was one tough lady. She stayed at Eagle Rock even though a lot of her neighbors wanted her out. Yesterday she seemed self-satisfied, even a little arrogant. She and Reverend McCall had a semipolite debate on the subject of spirits and conjurers. Undercurrents all over the place. Actually, I think Talia enjoyed it."

D.J. looked down at her quizzically. "A debate? Tell me exactly what was said."

Molly repeated the conversation as she remembered it.

"Did McCall seem upset?"

"Not too much. I think he felt he'd put Talia in her place."

As for Talia, her philosophy seemed to be live and let live, as she'd told Eva. *Well, it isn't the preacher's,* had been Eva's response. But of course Eva hadn't meant it literally, she hadn't meant that McCall wanted Talia dead. The idea was ludicrous.

"D.J.," Molly went on, "surely you're not thinking of the preacher as a suspect, if this turns out not to be suicide."

He shook his head. "Naw." He moved his shoulders to relieve the ache of tiredness. "So, how'd you like the wild onion breakfast?"

Molly hesitated and finally said, "The food was delicious, as usual."

He glanced down at her. "I detect a note of reservation in your tone. What happened?"

Molly had been vacillating over whether to tell him that Eva had heard from her father, and had finally concluded that now wasn't the time. He had enough on his mind and needed sleep. But since he'd asked the direct question, she couldn't avoid it.

"Grandmother heard from my father. He wants to see me."

His tired face lit up with a big grin. "Hey, that's great, sugar. When are you—" He halted, sensing her withdrawal. "It's not great?"

Molly leaned away from him, turned her head aside to look out the passenger window. "I don't know what it is, D.J."

"But I thought . . . well, I guess I figured you'd be thrilled to hear from him."

"Twenty years ago, even ten, I'd have been thrilled. Now I don't know what I feel." She swallowed to relieve a sudden tightness in her throat. "Grandmother thinks he's sick."

He studied her profile thoughtfully before he spoke. "And you think that's why he came back?"

"I don't know, but if he *is* sick, I have to wonder if that's the reason he came home." Her voice cracked. "What am I supposed to do about it?"

He placed his hand on her knee and squeezed gently. "Aren't you jumping the gun here? You haven't even talked to him. Maybe he only came back to see you."

Molly blew a strand of hair out of her eyes. "Kind of late for that, don't you think?"

"It's never too late, Molly. Give the guy a break."

She turned to gaze at him. "Give *him* a break?"

"Look, I know he ran off when you were a kid. But maybe he had a good reason."

"I can't imagine a reason good enough," she said stiffly.

"Listen, sweetheart, I don't want to argue with you. But you have no idea what happened before he left. You can bet he saw leaving as the only solution at the time. And you can bet it almost killed him to do it."

Good Lord, he was defending her father. Just like Eva.

"I'd really rather not talk about it right now, D.J."

She'd been awake half the night, thinking about her father, and still didn't know what to do. Oh, she knew she'd have to see him eventually. Only, this wasn't a good time, especially now that she was involved in what could be a murder investigation. And she sure didn't need Eva and D.J. criticizing her.

"Oo-kay," D.J. muttered.

As they approached the Eagle Rock compound, Molly saw the Sheriff's car parked on the grass in front of an old farmhouse with blooming forsythia bushes in front. It must be the Beaver home, since Hobart was standing on the porch, talking to the couple. A small knot of five or six people were gathered near the porch steps, listening to the exchange. Dell Greer was not among them.

D.J. parked behind the Sheriff's car and he and Molly got out and walked up to the porch steps.

"I'm gonna need statements from you people," the Sheriff was saying.

"We have nothing to say to the law," Agasuyed said sharply.

Ina Beaver, who stood beside the huge bulk of her husband, hanging on to his arm, said quietly, "What my husband means is that we know nothing about this. We're all sorry about Talia's death, but we can't help you."

"Sorry, are you?" Hobart snorted. "I hear you all wanted Talia Wind to move, tried to buy her out and when she wouldn't sell, somebody wrote her some nasty notes."

A young woman standing at the foot of the porch steps gasped and leaned over to whisper something to the older woman beside her. Molly watched the Beavers. Agasuyed's obstinate expression seemed to slip a little and something shifted behind his black eyes as he stared back at the Sheriff. Ina's hand on her husband's arm tightened, the bony fingers pressing into the soft flesh.

"I thought you said Talia killed herself," said a young, crew-cut man with the group.

"So?"

"If she did, those notes are sort of irrelevant, aren't they?"

Before the Sheriff could reply, Agasuyed said, "We don't know nothin' about no notes. I ain't even sure there were any notes. Talia might have *said* so, but she liked to stir up trouble."

A woman in the group next to the porch stepped forward.

She was the middle-aged woman who had been speaking to the younger woman. "Talia wouldn't lie about something like that," she said, shooting a defiant glance at Agasuyed. "Besides, she told me about the notes. They said she should leave or she'd be sorry. I didn't think she took them seriously enough, at least she didn't seem to." She glared at Agasuyed again. "Talia said only cowards write anonymous notes."

Agasuyed stared back at her, stone-faced, but Molly saw a glint of rage in his eyes. Ina looked at the floor.

The woman looked back at the Sheriff. "Talia was attacked, too. I don't think she got any more notes after that, but she stopped walking after dark. And she made me swear I would tell no one else about what had happened."

Molly edged around the woman and backed halfway up the porch steps. "When did this attack take place?"

The woman hesitated, looking from Molly to the Sheriff.

"This is Molly Bearpaw, an investigator for the Cherokee Nation," the Sheriff mumbled grudgingly.

"The attack happened two or three weeks ago," the woman said. "Between ten-thirty and eleven at night. Talia often took a walk around the compound at night, after the ten o'clock news." She pointed toward a stand of trees growing along the edge of the compound, next to the road. "Somebody hid in those trees and when Talia walked by, he jumped out and hit her. The next day her arm above the elbow was black-and-blue."

Hobart came down off the porch to stand a step above Molly, as though to take command of the questioning again. "What's your name?"

"Bessie Eyler. I was Talia's friend. Not everybody here wanted her to leave."

The other three women in the group nodded their agreement.

"Did Talia tell you who attacked her?"

Bessie Eyler hesitated, glanced at Agasuyed, and finally said reluctantly. "She didn't know. He came up on her from behind, and he ran back into the woods after he hit her. I don't think she saw him at all."

"Anybody else know anything about this attack?" the Sheriff demanded.

The only response was a unanimous shaking of heads.

Not bothering to modify the doubt in his voice, the Sheriff said, "Okay, but I still need statements. I want to know where everyone last saw Talia, if she seemed troubled or upset. It won't take long. Mr. and Mrs. Beaver, I'll talk to you first, inside the house if that's all right. D.J., you and Molly talk to these other people. I'll talk to Greer after I finish here."

Molly took the four women aside, leaving D.J. with the men. Two of the women, Andrea Fivekiller and Dolores Pruitt, were married to two men who were with the group, it turned out. The fourth woman was a young widow, Terri Luce. They were all involved in Talia's meditation groups. All four women had sided with Talia against Agasuyed Beaver.

Because the Fivekillers, the Pruitts, and the two single women lived closest to the Beavers, they had seen the Sheriff's car when it turned into the compound and had come over to investigate.

None of the women could tell Molly anything helpful to the investigation, except what she already knew, that Agasuyed and his followers, including Dell Greer, had wanted Talia out of the compound. Terri Luce had seen a car that looked like Talia's leave the compound the previous night sometime between eight and nine. Bessie Eyler was the only one of them who had known about the notes. Apparently Talia had confided in no one else at Eagle Rock, and she had sworn Bessie to secrecy.

"Did you see the notes?" Molly asked Bessie.

She shook her head. "Talia threw them out as soon as she got them. I think she only told me about them because I spent quite a bit of time with her and she needed to talk about it."

"Did she know who was sending them?"

"Only that it had to be somebody at Eagle Rock. The notes didn't come in the mail. They were slipped under her door while she was out. At first she thought it was Agasuyed," Bessie said, "but she couldn't prove it."

"At first? Had her opinion changed recently?"

"I think so. She didn't tell me, but I think she suspected it was Dell who attacked her, and that maybe he'd sent the notes, too."

"But you said she didn't see her attacker."

"She didn't. But Dell has been trying to buy her land and she kept refusing. The last time they talked, he got so mad she thought he was going to hit her. But he just cussed her and stomped off. The attack happened two nights later."

"Did he ever hit her when they were married?"

"Talia never said."

Molly wrote down names, addresses, and phone numbers and thanked the women. She stuffed her pad and pen into her shoulder bag. As the women turned away, she thought of another question and called Bessie Eyler back. "Where does Dell Greer live?"

Bessie pointed toward a small trailer. "The big mobile home closest to Dell's is Talia's."

"Does he still have access to Talia's mobile home?"

"No," Bessie said. "Talia had the locks changed. I'm the only other person who has a key. I helped Talia get ready for her groups."

"I'd like to look around Talia's place. Would you let me in?"

She thought about that for a moment. "I guess it's okay."

"Talia might have left a note in the trailer," Molly explained.

She cocked her head. "You believe it was suicide, too?"

"I really didn't know Talia well enough to have an opinion."

"Well, I did. Talia would never have killed herself."

Which seemed to be the opinion of all those who'd known Talia well. "A note would settle it once and for all."

"Okay. Come on. We'll have to go by my place for the key." Molly followed her out of the Beavers' yard. Looking back over her shoulder, Bessie Eyler added emphatically, "You won't find a suicide note, you'll see."

There shall remain but a trace upon the ground
where you have been.

9

"Look at these cards," D.J. said. He had picked up one of the decks on the coffee table in Talia Wind's mobile home and riffled through the cards. He held up one with an Indian shield on it. "What're these things for?"

"Readings, I think. Sort of like Tarot cards with a Native American twist."

D.J. put the cards down. "I thought Talia Wind was a traditional Cherokee conjurer."

"Not really. From what Natalie has said, Talia mixed Cherokee medicine with a lot of New Age stuff she learned in California."

"No wonder she and Agasuyed didn't get along," D.J. remarked, looking around the room. "Let's do a search. If we could find a suicide note, we could tie this thing up today."

"Bessie Eyler says it wasn't suicide."

"Maybe we'll find one of those anonymous notes."

"Bessie said Talia threw them away as soon as she received them."

D.J. gave a shrug. "Maybe Bessie doesn't know everything. I'll take the bedrooms, you look here and in the kitchen." He disappeared into a bedroom opening off the living room.

Molly searched the living room quickly. There were very few hiding places—under the couch and chair cushions and a couple of empty candy dishes with lids.

The kitchen took longer. She looked through all the cabinets and searched each drawer methodically, even looked in the canisters lined up on the countertop. Finally, she opened the doors beneath the sink and pulled out the wastebasket. It was empty except for a single piece of paper. The paper had been crumpled, but Molly could make out some words. She bent closer and read: GET OUT OF EAGLE ROCK. She couldn't see the rest. She started to reach in and pick up the paper, then thought better of it.

"Hey, D.J.," she called. "Look what I found."

He came in from the bedroom and leaned over her shoulder to read the visible words on the scrap of paper. "Bingo," he said and straightened up. "We'll need a search warrant if we ever want to use that in court. I'll tell the Sheriff."

"Maybe we'll get lucky and find some clear prints on it," Molly said.

He smiled. "What're the chances of that, do you think?"

"About a hundred to one against. And if Pohl says Talia committed suicide, it may not be worth pursuing the hate mail angle." She replaced the wastebasket and closed the cabinet door, looking at the peaceful setting outside. "She must have gotten that note very recently, probably Sunday. It's the only thing in her wastebasket."

"There's nothing interesting in the bedrooms," he said. "Let's go over to Dell Greer's."

They found Greer sitting on a redwood picnic table outside his trailer and talking to the Sheriff. Greer wore jeans and a thin white cotton T-shirt. His bare feet rested on a bench. His eyes were puffy and his black hair stood up in tufts. Clearly, the Sheriff had rousted him from his bed.

Hobart introduced D.J. and Molly, then said, "I guess that'll be all for now, Mr. Greer, but keep yourself available."

Greer threw him a disgruntled look. "I'm not going anywhere."

"Good thinking," said Hobart sarcastically and walked off. D.J. followed and the two men headed for the Sheriff's car, talking. Molly knew D.J. was telling Hobart about the note in Talia Wind's wastebasket.

"May I ask you a few questions, Mr. Greer?" Molly asked.

He stared at her belligerently, then threw one arm out. "Hell, go ahead. I got nothing to hide."

"Did you know that Talia had been receiving threatening notes?"

"I already told the Sheriff, and the answer is no."

"I work for the Cherokee Nation," Molly said. "I cooperate with the Sheriff's Department, but my investigation is independent of theirs. So, if you'll bear with me . . ."

He threw up both hands in a gesture of begrudging agreement.

"Did you know that Talia was recently attacked?"

He nodded. "At night, by those trees near the road. The Sheriff just told me. That was the first I heard of it."

"According to one of Talia's friends, she thought you did it."

His head jerked up. "Me? I never touched her. And, believe me, she gave me plenty of cause when we were married."

"Talia's friend says you were trying to buy her land."

"Everybody knows that. What's your point?"

"The friend says you were angry because Talia kept refusing. She says the last time you and Talia talked, you got so mad that Talia was afraid of you."

"Come on," he snorted. "I'll bet you've been talking to Bessie Eyler. The woman hates me. You wanta know the truth, I think she hates all men. She went through a bad divorce. But Talia was never afraid of me. Sure I got angry. Talia could make a saint lose his temper. She stayed at Eagle Rock out of plain pigheadedness. There was no other reason in the world for her to stay."

Molly glanced at the rear of Talia's mobile home where a vegetable and herb garden was bordered by red-blooming Japanese quince bushes. "I guess she liked it here. This was her home."

He didn't respond.

"Where were you Sunday night, from say, nine o'clock on?" Molly asked.

"Ran into town for a few minutes about midnight when I realized I was out of Skoal. I'm trying to quit smoking. Other than that, I was right here in my little home-sweet-home."

"Where did you buy the Skoal?"

"That all-night convenience store on Downy Street."

"How long would you say you were gone?"

"Not long, like I said. Ten, fifteen minutes, maybe."

"You came straight back here?"

"That's what I said," he retorted.

"Do you know anybody who can vouch for that?"

He shook his head. "Nope," he said defiantly. "Didn't see a soul except the store clerk when I went to town. Didn't even talk on the phone. Watched TV and went to bed."

Molly studied him. "Since you were here all night, except for those few minutes, you must have seen Talia leave for the library or heard her car."

"Nope," he said irritably and scratched his chin, which sported a night's growth of sparse black bristles. "Like I said, the TV was on. I didn't hear a thing. And I didn't make a habit of spying on my ex-wife." He yawned pointedly.

"You don't seem very broken up over Talia's death."

He shrugged, scratched his chin again. "The Sheriff said she was doing an exorcism in that library, trying to get rid of a ghost. Didn't surprise me. That's exactly the kind of squirrelly stuff Talia loved to get involved in. She was a kook, Miss Bearpaw. But I didn't wish her dead."

"It gets Talia out of Eagle Rock, though, doesn't it?"

He smiled tightly. "Can't deny that."

"Tell me something, Mr. Greer. Do you think Talia killed herself?"

For the first time, he seemed to take time to think about a question before answering. Leaning forward to rest his arms on his knees, he gazed down at his bare feet. When he looked up, he said, flippantly, "Looks like it, doesn't it?"

"Her niece and nephew don't believe it."

"Yeah, so the Sheriff said. Me, I don't know what to believe. I used to think I knew Talia, but I found out I didn't at all. And lately—" He shook his head. "She was always going on about getting in touch with the spirit world. Maybe she saw death as the best way in. Who knows?"

Molly was sure he didn't believe what he was saying, but his eyes were unreadable, his face slack and emotionless. "Thank you for your time, Mr. Greer," she said.

She felt his eyes on her back as she walked away.

The Sheriff had already gone back to town. D.J. was waiting for her beside his car. "Claude's going straight to the judge and ask for a search warrant."

"Good."

"What did Greer have to say for himself?"

"He was home all night Sunday night except for a short trip into town for Skoal. He didn't see or hear Talia leave home. She was crazy, and might have killed herself in a spiritual quest. He didn't write the notes. He didn't attack Talia."

"About what he told Claude."

"Does the Sheriff believe him?"

"At this point, he's just going through the motions. Claude is still counting on a suicide verdict. I had to press him to get him to ask for the warrant right away, before we hear from the ME."

Molly glanced toward the Beaver house. "Can you wait long enough for me to talk with the Beavers?"

"What's the point? They'll deny everything, just like Greer."

"Maybe they know nothing about any of this, but they'd say that to the Sheriff regardless. I find it hard to believe they're as ignorant as they claim. If Agasuyed didn't send the notes, he has a good idea who did. Maybe he'll open up a little more with me."

"Because you're one of his own." It was a statement, not a question. D.J. was a quarter-Cherokee himself, but the fact that he was an officer of the white man's law negated his Cherokee blood in the eyes of many traditional Cherokees. He opened the car door. "I'll wait for you out here." He got in, put his head back on the seat, and closed his eyes.

"Thanks. I won't be long."

Ina Beaver answered Molly's knock at the door. "Yes?"

"I need to ask you and your husband some questions, Mrs. Beaver."

Ina's weathered face hardened. "The Sheriff already did and wrote down the answers. Ask him."

"The Sheriff doesn't necessarily cooperate with the Nation. Please, Mrs. Beaver. Just give me a few minutes."

For a moment, Ina didn't move. Then, she reached out and opened the screen door. "A few minutes, but don't upset my husband. He's—" She hesitated. "He's under a doctor's care."

"I'm sorry," Molly said. "I'll be brief." She followed Ina Beaver through a living room furnished with a well-worn sofa and chairs, and a dining room with a heavy oak table and chairs, and into an old-fashioned, high-ceilinged kitchen with white cabinets and linoleum with a red-brick design. Agasuyed sat at a chrome dinette table, hunched over a syrup-smeared plate. He was drinking coffee from a giant mug.

He looked up, saw Molly, and glowered. "What's she doing here?" he snarled.

"I have to ask the two of you a few questions, Mr. Beaver."

He glared at her menacingly over the rim of his mug. "How come a Cherokee girl like you is doing the Sheriff's dirty work?"

"I don't work for the Sheriff. I work for the Cherokee Nation."

He banged his mug down, sloshing a little coffee on the table. "Don't matter to me." He made a sweeping motion with his hand, as if to dispense with all the Nation's employees in a single swoop.

"Agasuyed," Ina said soothingly, "let's just answer her questions so she can leave."

His fingers curled into fists. "She'll leave anytime I tell her to!"

"That's right," Molly said, "but I was hoping you'd cooperate with an employee of the Nation."

He picked up his mug again, gripping it tightly in both hands. His chins wobbled. "I'll save you some time. Me and Ina were home all yesterday afternoon and last night. I didn't send any threatening notes to Talia. I didn't jump out of the trees and hit her. I don't know when she left here last night." He stared at Molly belligerently. "Anything else?"

Molly turned to Ina Beaver. "What about you, Mrs. Beaver? Did you see or hear Talia's car when she left the compound last night?"

"I don't know anything about that." She said it quickly, her mouth snapping shut on the last word.

"All right. Thank you for talking to me."

Ina showed Molly out. At the door, Molly asked, "Mrs. Beaver, did Talia seem like the kind of person who might kill herself?"

She hesitated. "I guess any kind of person might if things got bad enough," she said.

"Did she seem different lately? More troubled? Depressed?"

"I wouldn't know. To tell you the truth, I didn't see much of Talia."

"Okay. Thanks again."

The door closed with a loud click. Molly looked at the graveled road which ran in front of the Beaver's house, bordering their front yard. It seemed to be the only way in or out of the compound. It was odd that neither of the Beavers had seen or heard Talia's car leaving last night. They were probably lying. But did they have a sinister motive or was it that they simply didn't want to get involved?

Molly trudged back to the patrol car and got in. D.J. stretched and lifted his head.

"You were right," she told him.

"Didn't spill their guts, huh?"

"No. They resent me as much as they resent the Sheriff. I think we should talk to some of the other residents of Eagle Rock."

D.J. started the engine. "Let's wait for the ME's report. We should get it tomorrow. Maybe it won't be necessary to talk to anybody else."

"I can't see Nat settling for suicide, no matter what Ken Pohl says."

"Nat will be okay. Give her time to get used to the idea."

The graveled road curved through blackjack oaks to a country road which was bordered by sumac bushes and redbud and wild plum trees. Molly caught only an occasional glimpse of an Eagle Rock dwelling through the trees. The settlement was nestled on low ground surrounded by wooded hills, like a bowl cupped in a protective hand. The conflicts among the residents seemed at odds with the peaceful setting.

They met no other cars until they neared the city limits

where shops and fast food restaurants slid by. "Do you want me to drop you at your office?" D.J. asked.

The question reminded Molly that she was without transportation. "Would you mind taking me out to Dowell's? I want to check on my car."

"Sure. They probably won't have it fixed yet, though."

"I know, but maybe I can hurry them along."

As they passed the library, she saw that her car was gone. When they reached the dealership, D.J. said, "I'll wait for you."

"No, you go home and get some rest."

"I've got the patrol car. You could use my car."

"Then you'd have to drive the patrol car off duty." Molly knew the Sheriff frowned on that. "Anyway, Tim said he could let me have a loaner if need be."

D.J. gazed at her for a long moment. "About your dad, Molly. Just give him a chance."

"I'll try." She bent over and kissed his cheek. "Catch you later." She got out of the car.

"Molly," he called as she was about to shut the door.

She stuck her head back inside.

"I love you."

She smiled. "And I love you."

On her way to the showroom, she saw a man walking across the used car lot, toward the library. He glanced at Molly and looked away quickly. It was Kurt Cloud, Deana's brother.

*Ha! You have put the Intruder into a crevice
in a high mountain and now the relief shall come.*

10

In the showroom, Molly strolled past a red Lexus, a black Prelude, and a couple of Accords, her mouth watering. Then she saw the suggested retail prices on their windows, which took her breath away. She contented herself with inhaling the new-car fragrance and, as no salesman appeared, she headed toward the back in search of the offices.

Tim Dowell's office door was open. He was leaning back in his chair, feet on the desk, talking on the telephone. In a red-plaid shirt and khakis with brown loafers, he looked like a model for L.L. Bean. He saw her, gave her a welcoming smile, and motioned for her to come in.

"That's fine, Mr. Merler," he was saying. "It's smart to compare prices. I don't think you can beat ours, though." He covered a yawn with his hand. Then, "You think it over and let me know." He hung up, slid his loafers off the desk, and unfolded his six feet plus. "Hi, Molly."

"Tim. Thanks for towing my car."

"Sure. Sit down."

He waited until Molly settled into one of the chairs facing his desk before flopping back into his own chair.

"Has the mechanic had a chance to look at the car?"

He sat back, laced his fingers on his chest, his thumbs touching. He looked like a man who was about to deliver bad news. "He's not finished yet, but he already told me there's a leak in your oil pan. That's no big deal. But you've got a cracked piston, too, and that is."

Molly groaned. "How much will it cost to fix it?"

"For a new oil pan and piston alone, it comes to eight hundred. That's mostly for the piston and labor. For you, I can knock off fifty bucks, but we don't know what else he'll find."

Now she had a new dilemma. There was a good chance the Civic was worth less than what it would cost to repair it, but she had to have transportation. She could get four hundred from her bank account, and she'd have to charge the rest to her Visa card and pay the high interest.

"When will you know the full story?"

"Tomorrow morning probably. With what we know so far, the repair could take a week. Gotta order parts."

Molly nodded glumly. "About that loaner . . ."

He grinned. "I already told the guys to check it over." He grabbed the phone and dialed. "Hardy, you looked at that '87 Accord yet? Good. Bring it around front, will ya?" He replaced the receiver. "If you like it, we can work out easy payments for you."

"I'll have to think about it."

He yawned again. "Sorry. It's been a long morning. I need coffee. You got time for a cup?"

"I could use one. Black, please."

He left for a few moments and returned with two full Styrofoam cups. He set his cup on the desk and sagged back into his chair. "Awful, what happened at the library."

"Did you know Talia Wind?"

He shook his head.

Molly blew on her coffee and took a sip. It was fresh and just strong enough, the way she liked it.

"Deana Cloud thinks the ghost is to blame."

He chuckled. "Naturally."

"Speaking of Deana," Molly said. "I saw her brother skulking through your parking lot as I came in. Kurt Cloud. You know him?"

Tim wobbled his hand in the air. "I know who he is. Kind of a sad case."

"He was probably walking through on his way to the library to see his sister, but you might want to keep an eye out for him. He spent some time in prison on a burglary conviction."

"Yeah, I know. In fact, he was leaving here when you saw him. He came to see me, looking for a job. He took an auto mechanics course in prison."

"You sure he wasn't casing the joint?" Molly asked, only half-jokingly.

He smiled and shook his head. "He says he's off drugs, wants to stay off. Seemed sincere."

"They always are when they want something." Molly realized how cynical she sounded and wondered if her job was making her hard. Maybe, and maybe she'd just gotten realistic.

"I feel sorry for him," Tim said. "But right now I don't have an opening. I promised to let him know when I do."

Molly liked the way he looked you straight in the eye when

he was talking to you. And she liked his seeming willingness to think the best of people, even if in this case it was probably a bit naive. "Did you mean it?"

He seemed surprised by the question. "I wouldn't have said it if I didn't. If a con is serious about going straight, somebody has to be willing to hire him."

Molly couldn't argue with that. While most people would agree with Tim in theory, they didn't want to hire convicts *themselves.* "True." She took a long swallow of coffee, set her cup on the corner of his desk. She cleared her throat. "D.J. Kennedy mentioned you had a little problem with your dad last night."

He raised an eyebrow and said morosely, "Scared the hell out of me. I woke up about five and went to look in on him, and he was gone. He could've been gone for hours. It's not unusual for him to wander around the house at night, and a few times I've found him in the yard. But he never wandered so far before, and I always heard him until last night. Took some paperwork home over the weekend, worked till late last night. I was so tired by the time I got to bed, I just died. Didn't hear a thing. Dad could have fallen and broken a leg, wandered out onto the highway in front of a car—anything." He shuddered. "I scared myself with all kinds of horror stories while we were looking for him. Then the deputies found him stretched out on a picnic table, sleeping like a baby."

"Was he frightened?"

"Didn't seem to be." He shook his head uncomprehendingly. "When they brought him home, he just looked at me and said, 'Oh, there you are. I was looking for you,' went to his room and crawled into bed." His brow furrowed with worry as he reached for his coffee cup and drained it.

"Have you thought about a good nursing home?"

He set his cup down and gripped the arms of his chair. "Yeah, I've thought about it. But he'd have to get a lot worse before I could put him away."

"That's not exactly putting him away. You could still see him every day."

"He's my father," he said simply. "He would've done anything for me before—before he got the way he is. He gave me his house and turned over the dealership to me. Dad worked hard building up this place, and it's been a good business. I can't put him somewhere with strangers and forget about him." He looked away from her, as though he'd embarrassed himself by exposing his feelings.

"He's lucky to have a son like you."

"I'm lucky to have a dad like him," he said, his tone solemn. "Some of my happiest memories are things I did with Dad, growing up. We used to take some great camping trips."

"You know something? I envy you," she told him. "My dad wasn't around when I was growing up."

He sat forward, rested his elbows on the desk, as if glad to turn the conversation away from himself and his loyalty to his father. "That must have been tough for you."

"Yeah."

"Did you get to see him much?"

"I didn't see him at all." Almost before Molly realized it, she was telling him about her father's desertion, her mother's suicide, her father's return, and her reluctance to face him.

He listened attentively, nodding now and then.

Finally, she started to listen to herself and was appalled.

She was not the sort to confide in strangers. Tim Dowell was an unusually sympathetic listener. "I'm sorry," she apologized.

"What for?"

"I shouldn't have dumped all that on you."

"It's okay. Sometimes it helps just to talk."

She was embarrassed. "You must think I'm hard-hearted because I'm not jumping at the chance to see my father."

"Not at all." He surprised her by reaching out and patting her hand, which rested on his desk. "Hey, Molly, don't put a guilt trip on yourself. I understand how you feel. If I were in your shoes I'd probably feel the same way."

She doubted that, but she was grateful. "Thanks for listening."

"Anytime. Can I make just one suggestion?"

She smiled. "Sure."

"The longer you put off seeing your father, the harder it will be. Why don't you get it over with? It might turn out better than you imagine. Think about it, okay?"

"I have been."

He rose. "Come on. I'll walk you out to the car."

The Accord was light brown (sandalwood, according to Tim), with a fresh wash and wax job. "This is great," she said. "I'll take good care of it." She opened the door and got in. The interior, also brown, was spotlessly clean, the upholstery hardly worn at all.

He caught the door as it was closing. "Molly." He looked suddenly shy. "Would you like to go to dinner sometime?"

She hadn't been expecting it and felt warmth creeping up her throat. "I'd like to, Tim, but I can't. I'm sort of involved with someone."

His face fell, but he smiled good-naturedly. "D.J. Kennedy?"

She nodded.

"I heard tell," he said. "But you can't blame a guy for trying. Kennedy's a lucky man." He shut the car door firmly and waved as she drove away.

She was ridiculously flattered. Tim Dowell was a nice man. If she weren't involved with D.J., she would definitely like to know him better.

Thinking of D.J. made her feel uncomfortable. Now why was that? It was a moment before she had the answer.

Why couldn't she talk to D.J. about her father, yet could discuss her feelings with a man she'd just met? Then, she thought she knew why. D.J. seemed too eager to jump to her father's defense.

Back at her office, Molly couldn't get Tim Dowell's advice out of her mind. He was right, of course. Before she could change her mind, she called her grandmother.

"Hi. It's me."

"I was going to call you. Rob called again last night. I told him what you said."

Molly fingered the turtle paperweight. "How'd he take it?"

"He said he understands how you feel, but he still wants to see you."

"When do you think he'll call again?"

"Tonight, he said."

"Well, I've made a decision. Tell him I'll meet him at The Shack tomorrow evening at seven." She would buy his dinner, or go dutch if he insisted. She didn't want him paying for her meal.

Eva hesitated. "Not at your apartment?"

"I don't think so."

"You could come here. I could go next door for a while."

Molly wasn't sure why, but she felt it would be easier if they weren't alone. "No, Grandmother. I'd rather meet him at the café."

"Okay, if that's the way you want it."

"Thanks, Grandmother."

Molly started to hang up when Eva said, "Molly . . ."

"Yes?"

"You know that I've always done what I thought was best for you, don't you?"

"Of course I do, Grandmother. What are you getting at?"

"Nothing. I'll talk to you later."

Molly replaced the receiver, feeling an odd mixture of anxiety and relief. The die was cast. Tomorrow evening she would see her father. The waiting, at least, would be over.

She took a few deep breaths before picking up the phone again. She left word for the Medical Examiner to call her as soon as he'd done the autopsy on Talia Wind.

Later, she called the Sheriff's office and was told that a search warrant for Talia Wind's mobile home had been issued and that the Sheriff had gone back out to Eagle Rock.

It would be a break if the note yielded some hard evidence, Molly thought as she hung up. She leaned back in her chair and looked out the window, beyond the square, to Muskogee Avenue, where the traffic was brisk. Was her father in one of the cars passing on the street?

*   *   *

It was Tuesday morning before Ken Pohl got back to her.

"Come by my office and pick up the autopsy report," Pohl said. "I gave one to the Sheriff and made a copy for you."

"I will," Molly said, "but give me the short version now."

"The short version, eh? Always in a fizz, aren't you Molly? Have I mentioned that you'll get ulcers if you don't learn to relax?"

Molly bit back a sharp retort. She was feeling testy, but that wasn't Pohl's fault. She hadn't slept, had lain awake for hours worrying about the meeting with her father. Would she recognize him? Would he recognize her? What on earth would she say to him?

"Several times," Molly said in reply to Pohl's question, doubting that the doctor would ever have ulcers. He actually enjoyed his grisly job. She didn't doubt for a second that he could eat a sandwich with one hand while examining a corpse with the other, should he choose to. "But I have a personal stake in this one, Doc. The victim's niece works for me."

"I see. Well, the short version is that the rope marks on Talia Wind's neck are inconsistent with death from hanging. The angle's all wrong. In a gallows hanging, death results from fracture-dislocation of the upper spinal vertebrae. Furthermore, the face wasn't pale, as it probably would have been from death by hanging. Besides which—" He paused, as if preparing to deliver a zinger. "—the imprints from the rope were postmortem."

Wow. He could have said that and skipped the rest, but then Pohl got a kick out of stringing her along. "You're saying she was dead when she was put on the gallows?"

"Exactly. And I'd swear to it in court."

"Then how *did* she die?"

"There are bruises indicating manual strangulation. And her face was congested, with a lot of ruptured blood vessels, which is what occurs in a ligature strangulation."

"Can you say how much time elapsed between death and the rope being strung around her neck?"

"I'd guess no more than a few minutes."

Molly let this new information sink in. Talia Wind had been murdered. This wasn't really what she had wanted to hear. "What's your estimate as to time of death?"

"She was in full rigor when I first saw her. Based on that plus body temperature at the time she arrived at the morgue, which was nine o'clock Monday morning, and the fact that it got down to about forty degrees Sunday night, I'd say she'd been dead between five and eight hours."

That put time of death at between one and four A.M. Sunday morning. "So Natalie and Ridge were right."

"Who?"

"Talia Wind's niece and nephew. They insisted that Talia wouldn't kill herself." Molly opened a desk drawer and took a Snickers bar from her emergency rations. She had finally fallen asleep about three A.M., and then she'd overslept and hadn't had time for breakfast. She'd barely had time to feed Homer. Fortunately, she had taken him for a long walk last night.

She peeled back the wrapper while she thought. "How'd the Sheriff take the news?"

Pohl chuckled. "He's not a happy camper."

Molly smiled and prepared to take a bite of the Snickers. "Thanks, Doc. I'll run by and pick up that report today or tomorrow."

"One other finding you might be interested in."

She had already taken the receiver away from her ear. She clamped it back in place. "What?"

"The lady had sex not too long before her death."

"Was she raped?"

"No indication of forced entry."

"Hmm. Well, thanks again, Doc." She hung up and settled back in her chair to finish the candy bar.

Who had Talia been with before she died? Natalie had said she thought Talia was seeing someone, but she was being secretive about it. Which could mean several things. Talia didn't want Greer to know about it, perhaps for fear that he'd confront the man. Or maybe the man was married.

Finishing the Snickers, she tossed the wrapper into the wastebasket beside her desk. As she did so, the door swooshed open and Natalie rushed in.

"You shouldn't be here," Molly said. "You shouldn't try to work today. It's too soon, Nat."

Natalie's hair lacked its customary shine—clearly she'd skipped her regular morning shampoo. There were dark smudges beneath her eyes. And her jeans and green NSU T-shirt looked as if they'd been slept in.

Natalie planted her hands on Molly's desk and leaned forward, demanding breathlessly, "Have you heard?"

"What?"

"Aunt Talia was murdered!"

"Oh. Yes, I just talked to the Medical Examiner. How'd you find out so fast?"

"Ridge camped outside the Sheriff's office until Hobart told him the results of the autopsy. So, what now?"

"Now, the Sheriff and I conduct a murder investigation."

Natalie straightened up, planted her hands on her hips. "What can I do?"

"Shouldn't you be in class?"

She shook her head. "Couldn't concentrate."

"Nat, you look like you need some sleep. Why don't you go back to the dorm and rest?"

Red spots appeared on Natalie's pale cheeks. "You expect me to sleep when Aunt Talia has been murdered?"

Molly refrained from remarking on the absurdity of the remark. Did Natalie plan to stay awake until the murderer was caught? "Okay, then, you could spend some time with your parents."

She whirled and walked over to her desk and leaned back against it, bracing herself with both hands. "I'll see them before they leave. They're going back home to Idabel this afternoon to make arrangements for Talia's funeral. It'll be Thursday or Friday. We're her only close relatives."

Molly thought of something she'd wondered about last night. "What's going to happen to her car and the property at Eagle Rock?"

"She made a new will after the divorce. Had it notarized and witnessed and mailed a copy to Dad. She left the car and the money from the sale of her tapes to him and the property to Ridge and me." Her mouth twisted scornfully. "Neither of us would live out there on a bet, so we'll sell it."

"Dell Greer has been trying to buy it."

She pushed herself away from the desk, walked back to stand in front of Molly. "No way. I think he killed her. I'll bet he doesn't know about the new will. The old one, made when they were married, left everything to him."

"The Beavers then . . ."

"I hope we don't have to sell to them, either. If Dell didn't kill Aunt Talia, then Agasuyed did."

"I wouldn't broadcast these accusations if I were you. Slander can get you in trouble."

"It's not slander if it's true!"

"There's no evidence linking either Greer or Agasuyed Beaver to the murder."

"Not yet," she said stubbornly. "Now, tell me what I can do to help with the investigation."

Molly considered refusing, but decided to make one more stab at common sense. "I know it's hard to concentrate on your classes, but don't you need to study for finals?"

"How can I think about *school* at a time like this?" Natalie asked incredulously. "I can pass three of my courses without cracking a book, anyway. I'll take an I in the other two and make it up later."

Molly started to argue, looked at the stubborn set to Natalie's mouth, and decided to save her breath. Instead, she said, "You said Talia was seeing someone. You sure you don't know who it was?"

She shook her head. "She wouldn't tell me. In fact, she denied that she was even involved with anyone when I asked. Why?"

It seemed obvious that the Sheriff hadn't told Ridge everything the autopsy revealed—he hadn't mentioned that Talia had had sex not long before her death.

"We need to talk to him," Molly said. "We need to talk to everybody who was close to Talia."

Natalie thought about it. "I'll see if Ridge or Dad knows anything, but I don't think so. In the meantime, you have to let me do something to help, Molly. I *need* to do this for Aunt Talia. If I have to, I'll go out on my own."

Great. Just what she needed, Molly thought, Natalie on her own personal vendetta. Well, maybe Natalie would be better off doing *something*. And Molly wanted to stay busy today, too. It might keep her from worrying about meeting her father.

She waved toward Natalie's desk. "Sit down for a minute and let me think about it."

The Intruder is sent to the Darkening Land.
You have put it to rest in the Darkening Land.
Let the relief come.

11

Molly decided not to wait for the Sheriff to decide when he was going back to Eagle Rock. Hobart did grudgingly give her more information on the threatening note he'd retrieved from Talia's mobile home. They had found several blurred prints, but none clear enough to identify. The crumpled note they found at the bottom of the wastebasket said it was Talia's last warning and that she'd be sorry if she didn't heed it. From what Bessie Eyler had said, the warning was similar to the previous ones, except for that "last warning" bit, which sounded ominous.

It seemed to tie the note writer to the killing, except for one thing. He, or she, hadn't given Talia much time to comply—if Molly's theory was correct and Talia received the note sometime Sunday.

It was mid-morning when Molly and Natalie arrived at the compound. "It's really pretty out here," Natalie said, her voice trembly. "I can see why Aunt Talia wanted to stay. I wouldn't mind living here myself if she wasn't—gone."

"You sure you want to do this?"

"Absolutely."

Molly parked near the Beaver house. "There are only about a dozen houses here. We'll split up and knock on every door."

Natalie climbed out of the car. "Where do you want me to start?" She blinked in the bright sunlight and squared her shoulders.

Molly had no intention of turning Natalie loose on the Beavers and Dell Greer. She wanted them for herself. "Start at the far end," Molly said, indicating the two-lane graveled road that wound through the settlement. "I'll take it from here and we'll meet in the middle."

"Got it," Natalie said grimly and started off.

"Wait!"

Natalie turned back.

"You sure you know what to do?" Molly had spent half an hour priming Natalie for the questioning.

"It's engraved up here." She tapped her forehead. "Trust me, Molly."

That was exactly what Molly was having trouble with. No one so emotionally involved in a case should take part in the investigation.

Molly was still reluctant to let her go. "You've got your questions?" She had given Natalie a list of the questions she wanted answered.

Natalie patted the pocket of her jeans. "Right here, along with my trusty pad and pen." She smiled wryly. "Can I go now, Captain?"

Molly couldn't think of further delaying tactics. "Go on, get out of here."

Natalie saluted and trotted off, full of righteous determination to ferret out the truth.

Glancing at the Beaver house, Molly decided to save it for last. She headed for Dell Greer's travel trailer. Greer was puttering around outside. If she'd had to live in Greer's claustrophobic little trailer, she thought she'd spend as much time as possible outside, too. Her apartment was basically one room with a kitchenette, but it had three or four times the square footage of Greer's trailer.

The air smelled of new-mown grass and Greer, in jeans cutoffs and a faded orange T-shirt, was bending over a manual lawn mower with a spouted oil can in one hand. At the moment, he didn't look like a man who'd recently squeezed the life out of his ex-wife, but Molly knew how deceiving looks can be.

"Mr. Greer?"

He straightened up, his questioning expression turning to a frown when he recognized her. "You again?" he mumbled churlishly.

"There's been a new development in Talia's case, and I need to talk to you."

He deposited the oil can on the frame of the mower and faced her, feet in run-over walking shoes, planted a foot apart. "What new development?"

"She didn't die of hanging. She was strangled before she was put on the gallows." His surly expression hardly changed, just a twitch of a muscle beside his mouth. Hoping for more of a reaction, she clarified, "It was murder, Mr. Greer."

He studied her suspiciously. No sign of remorse or even

much surprise from the man who had been married to Talia until recently. "I always knew Talia's hard head would get her in trouble sooner or later."

"What do you mean?"

"Talia went her own way. She wouldn't listen to common sense, caution—nothing. Being married to the woman was no picnic."

"So you both wanted the divorce?"

He looked at his hands, wiped a smudge of grease off on his cutoffs, and stuffed his fingers into his hip pockets. He glanced at Molly. "I'd have stuck it out, but Talia wouldn't have it. She was hard to live with, sure, but one thing you could say for Talia—she was never boring."

"You still loved her."

It wasn't a question, and if Greer took it as one, he chose not to answer. "What's all this got to do with Talia's murder?"

"That should be obvious."

He snorted contemptuously. "Why don't you spell it out for me, anyway."

"From what I hear, your divorce left hard feelings on both sides. You admit you didn't want it in the first place. Furthermore, spouses and ex-spouses are always the first ones the police look at in a murder investigation."

"They can look all they want. They won't get anything on me 'cause I wasn't there." He pulled his fingers out of his pockets and reached for the oil can, turning his back to Molly. "I don't have time for this. I've got work to do."

"Did you know Talia was involved in a—um, romantic relationship?"

He jerked around. "How do you know that?"

"Her niece told me."

His lips thinned into a straight line, then he shook his head. "Talia was free to do whatever she wanted." But his voice was tight.

"You didn't know she was seeing someone?"

"No. And I wouldn't have done anything about it if I had. She wasn't my wife anymore." He turned away.

Molly didn't believe him. The idea that Talia was involved with another man didn't sit well, and she thought he'd known about the other man before she told him and he was jealous. How long had he known? He could easily have followed Talia Sunday night and seen her meet the other man.

"Did you know she'd made a new will?" Molly asked.

He whirled around again, one hand gripping the oil can. "I don't know—or care—anything about Talia's business or who she associated with since the divorce." But clearly, he was shaken by something she'd said. Was Natalie right about Greer's assuming the old will was still in effect, the one leaving everything to him? He and Talia had been divorced only a few months, and people tend to put off things like making new wills.

"She left her property to her niece and nephew."

"Oh?"

"Thought you'd like to know, since you've been trying to buy it."

"Correction. Agasuyed Beaver wanted to buy it. I was just acting as his agent. Now that Talia's not here anymore, I doubt Beaver will want the property."

Molly let her gaze fall on his trailer. "Pretty cramped quarters you've got here."

"What's it to you?" he asked belligerently.

"It just occurred to me. If Mr. Beaver should buy Talia's

property, he'd have no use for the mobile home. You could probably get it for a song."

He shook his head, as if at her ignorance. "You can buy used trailer houses anywhere around here cheap. Check the want ads." He turned his back and began squirting oil on a mower wheel.

Molly left, making a mental note to stop at the convenience store where Greer claimed he'd bought chewing tobacco Sunday night. She knocked on more doors, working her way toward the Beaver house.

Four brief interviews later, she'd come up with little more than she'd already known. Everybody she talked to was aware of Agasuyed Beaver's efforts to force Talia out of Eagle Rock, but they all seemed genuinely shocked to learn that Talia had been murdered. Several women in Talia's meditation groups expressed outrage and the hope that the killer would be caught quickly. Only Terri Luce would admit to seeing Talia leave the compound Sunday night. Molly didn't think Talia had gone straight to the library. She'd met her lover first. But who was he? And where had they met?

Bessie Eyler opened her door before Molly had a chance to knock. "I saw you coming up the walk," she said. "Come on in."

She offered Molly a cold drink, which Molly declined. They sat in Bessie's small, neat living room. She cried and left the room when Molly told her that Talia had been murdered. When she came back, her eyes were red, but she'd stopped sobbing.

She sat back down on the couch. "Who could have hated Talia enough to kill her?"

"We know there was no love lost between her and the

Beavers. And her ex-husband just told me he didn't want the divorce. It was Talia who insisted on it."

She dabbed at her red eyes with a tissue. "Oh, I know that, but I can't believe any of them would actually kill her."

"You seemed to have no trouble believing that Dell Greer attacked her with a club."

She thought about that for a moment. "Dell has a temper. I can believe he might have gotten mad and hit her, but kill her?" She shook her head, then stopped abruptly. "Unless she got him really mad and he acted without thinking, not really meaning to kill her." She frowned. "Yes, I can see that."

Molly could imagine Greer getting "really mad" when he'd learned that Talia had a lover.

"And Agasuyed Beaver?"

Bessie tilted her head. "This is strange, trying to decide which of your neighbors might be a murderer." She paused, then, "I know Agasuyed's been making medicine meant to make Talia leave Eagle Rock. He's made no secret of it. Do you think one of his followers could have decided to help Agasuyed out by killing Talia?"

"You'd have a better idea about that than I. Anybody in particular come to mind?"

"No." She paused and seemed to shake herself. "I can't believe Agasuyed did it—or even caused somebody else to do it. You don't kill somebody, no matter how much you don't want them for a neighbor anymore."

There was much more to it than a disagreement among neighbors, and Molly was sure Bessie knew that. "Talia was involved with a man," she said.

Bessie looked up, startled. "How did you know that?"

"Talia's niece told me."

"Did she tell you who he is?"

Molly shook her head. "She doesn't know. I thought you might."

Bessie clasped her hands, lifted them and gnawed absently on a knuckle for an instant. Finally, she said, "I knew she'd met someone a few times. She didn't talk about it, but she was in love, happier than I'd ever seen her. It was written all over her." She wiped away a tear with the tissue. "I don't think it had been going on long, maybe a couple months."

"Did he ever come here?"

"Not that I know of."

"Do you know where they met?"

She shook her head.

"Did Talia ever suggest that Dell Greer knew about it?"

Again, Bessie shook her head.

"I need to know his name, Bessie. We have to know everything we can about Talia if we're going to catch the killer."

She gnawed the knuckle again, then dropped her hands. "Josh," she said. "Talia slipped once and said his name. Just Josh. I don't know his last name. That's the only time she ever mentioned him to me."

Josh . . . The name rang a bell. Then Molly remembered the wild onion breakfast at the Indian Baptist Church and the look that had passed between Talia and the man Eva had said was a church deacon, a married church deacon. Josh Rollins.

After a few more minutes, she thanked Bessie and left. As she went down Bessie's front walk, she saw a boy about nine or ten years old riding his bike down the graveled road. He stopped, watching her approach curiously.

"Hi," Molly said.

"Hi. I'm Eddie."

"Glad to meet you, Eddie. I'm Molly."

"You been to see Bessie?"

"That's right."

"She's nice."

"Yes, she is."

"She gives me cookies."

"Where do you live?"

He pointed down the road at a house where Molly had already stopped. She'd talked to the woman inside, evidently this boy's mother. He was skinny, his legs and arms like sticks, with close-cropped hair and a pug nose. "Why aren't you in school?"

"I go to home school. My mom teaches me. She used to be a teacher. She thinks she can do a better job than the regular school. She says they don't challenge me enough."

He seemed like a bright boy. Molly could understand his mother wanting him to be challenged, but she wondered if depriving him of the social interaction he'd have in school was worth the trade-off.

"What do you think?" she asked.

"I think I'd rather go to the regular school. All the other kids out here go to school in town."

"So you're the only kid out here on school days."

He nodded. "I usually finish my lessons by noon, and there's not much to do after that till the school bus comes. I play computer games or ride my bike, sometimes I work on my stamp collection or go fishing."

"I'll bet you know more about what goes on around here than almost anybody."

He grinned. "Yeah, but not much goes on."

"Did you know Talia Wind?"

His expression turned very serious. "The lady who died?" Molly nodded. "I knew her," he went on. "Everybody knows everybody out here. She was kind of weird, but nice."

"Did you see her Sunday?"

He gave it some thought. "I saw her in the morning, getting in her car. She had on a real pretty dress."

"Yes, she was going to church. Did you see her after that? Around her mobile home? Or in her car?"

"No, just Mrs. Beaver."

"She was probably going to church, too," Molly mused, trying to think of other questions to ask the boy.

"Not when I saw her. She was on the porch, and she had on some old pants, so I don't think she was going to church."

He'd seen Ina Beaver on her porch sometime Sunday. Nothing unusual about that. This was getting her nowhere, Molly thought, glancing toward the Beaver house.

"She knocked," the boy went on, "but nobody answered. The lady had already left in her car."

Molly turned around. "Wait a minute. Whose porch was Mrs. Beaver on when you saw her?"

"The lady who died. Over there." He pointed toward Talia's mobile home.

Despite her denial, Ina Beaver had probably seen Talia's car go by the Beaver house, so why had she come to call on Talia? Besides, Molly had gotten the impression that the Beavers were hardly on speaking terms with Talia.

Molly bent over a little and looked him in the eyes. "Eddie, this is important. Are you sure it was Sunday when you saw Mrs. Beaver on Talia's porch?"

He nodded gravely.

"Did Mrs. Beaver do anything else—besides knock on Talia's door, I mean?"

He kicked at a bike pedal to reposition it. "Not really. She just walked down the road and up to the mobile home and knocked on the door. Then she bent over for a minute, and then she left and went back home."

"Bent over?"

He reached down to adjust the pedal. "Yeah, like she was tying her shoe or something."

"Thank you, Eddie. You've been very helpful."

He pedaled off. "Bye," he called over his shoulder.

She continued toward the Beaver house, pondering what the boy had told her. Ina had said that she didn't see much of Talia. What could have sent her to Talia's mobile home Sunday, and why hadn't she mentioned it when the Sheriff and Molly questioned her? Could be a lot of reasons, Molly guessed. Maybe she didn't want Agasuyed to know about it, for instance.

It was, she told herself, entirely possible that Ina Beaver had been tying her shoe when Eddie saw her bend over.

It was also possible she'd gone to Talia's, knowing Talia wasn't there, knocked just to be double sure, and then had bent over to slip something under Talia's door.

Struck by the thought, Molly halted several yards short of the Beavers' yard. Quiet, retiring Ina Beaver delivering threatening notes to Talia? It didn't exactly fit Molly's impression of the woman. She seemed to defer to her husband in most things.

So, maybe Agasuyed sent her with the note. And, if so, Agasuyed had written it. But why the notes, when he intended to drive Talia away with medicine ceremonies?

Listen! Ha! Now you have drawn near to hearken, O Blue Raven;
you are resting directly overhead.

12

"Eddie got Ina mixed up with somebody else," Agasuyed Beaver said. They were standing on his front porch. He'd stepped out rather than ask Molly to come in, and he'd left the front door open, a quick retreat route. He claimed Ina had gone to the grocery store, which was probably true, as Molly had already noted that the Chevrolet was gone. "Must've been one of those women who go over there for readings. Ina and me haven't been near Talia's place in weeks."

"Eddie's sure it was Ina," Molly said.

"And I'm sure it wasn't," Agasuyed growled. "Now, get off my porch." He stepped back inside and shut the door in Molly's face.

Molly went back to the Accord and waited for Natalie, who showed up ten minutes later.

Molly started the car, glancing at Natalie's downcast face. "Still clueless, right?"

Natalie gave her a grimace of a smile. "They're like those three monkeys," she said. "See nothing, hear nothing, speak nothing."

"I think that's see no evil, and so on."

"Whatever. It comes down to the same thing." She laid her head back against the seat. "Anyway, it has to be Dell or Agasuyed who killed her. Did you talk to them?"

"Yes, but neither of them seems overcome by guilt," Molly said dryly. "They didn't break down and confess, at any rate."

"We just have to prove they're guilty, that's all."

"Both of them?"

"You know what I mean. One or the other, and I'm betting on Agasuyed. There's a real mean look in that man's eyes." She lifted her head and shifted in the seat to face Molly. "Maybe we could plant a bug in his house."

"Great idea," Molly said mildly. "Unfortunately, it's against the law."

Natalie didn't want to hear picky little things about the law. She rolled her dark eyes. "Like killing Aunt Talia isn't."

"Don't be absurd, Nat," Molly said. "Even if we could bug the Beaver house, even if we got Agasuyed on tape saying he killed Talia, it would be thrown out of court. You know that as well as I do. *You're* the one who's planning to be a lawyer, for heaven's sake."

Natalie didn't answer, just leaned her head against the window and sighed. Molly wished she could think of something encouraging to say to Natalie, but nothing came to mind, nothing she wanted to share with Natalie, anyway.

"I guess I better go by Ridge's and see my folks before they leave town," Natalie said.

Molly drove back toward Cherokee Square where Natalie

had left her car, hoping that their visit to Eagle Rock had made Natalie realize she couldn't be much help in the investigation.

As Molly pulled up beside Natalie's car, Natalie said, "Tell me something, Molly. Is it true that criminals go back to the scene of the crime?"

"Sometimes. I guess." She scrutinized Natalie's tired face. "Wait a minute. You're not thinking of doing something stupid, are you?"

"No." Natalie opened the car door and stepped out. "Merely asking a simple question. See ya." She slammed the door and got into her own car.

Driving away from the square, Molly rolled down the driver's side window. The morning breeze was laden with the faint scent of lilacs from the bushes in several yards along the streets which angled off Muskogee Avenue. She passed the corner where the Computamax store used to be, where she'd bought her books and rented videos. But it had gone out of business. Now the building housed the Cherokee Cultural Center.

A little farther along was the building where her friend Moira Pack had worked until recently. Late last year, Moira had married a young attorney, Bruce Hilldebrand, who'd been working for Moira's boss. A couple months ago Moira and Bruce had moved to Sallisaw, where Bruce had opened his own law office. Molly missed having Moira right down the street from her office.

She braked for a stop light. The remnants of a glazed doughnut lay at the edge of the sidewalk in front of Morgan's Bakery next to The Shack, where Molly would meet her father that evening. But she didn't want to think about that, so she focused on a crow and several blue jays, who were hopping off and on the curb vying for the biggest piece of doughnut. The crow ducked in among the jays, grabbed a piece, and hopped away.

The driver behind Molly honked at her. She hadn't noticed that the light was green. She accelerated, turning on Downey Street.

She parked in front of the only convenience store on the street that stayed open all night. The clerk was a woman. Her eyes and nose were red, and she was breathing through her mouth. "Allergies," she explained and blew her nose.

Molly introduced herself and asked who had been working the counter Sunday night. "That'd be my old man, Johnny. We own the store. Hold on a sec—" She held a tissue to her nose and sneezed three times in quick succession. "Sorry, but there's something in the air." She gestured toward the door. "Happens every time somebody comes in. Now what was I saying?"

"About Sunday night . . ."

"Oh, yeah. We got a guy who usually works nights, but he was sick Sunday so Johnny had to fill in."

"I'd like to ask your husband a couple of questions."

The woman squinted at her. "What about?"

"It has to do with the investigation of a crime. I can't say any more than that."

The woman studied her, then said, "Johnny's here now." She jerked her head toward the swinging doors at the back of the store as a customer came in. "He's got a little office there. You can go on back." Then she clamped a tissue to her nose and sneezed.

Molly pushed through the swinging doors and made her

way around cardboard boxes and empty soft drink crates to the small room partitioned off in a back corner. The door was open, revealing a man seated at a battered desk, writing in an old-fashioned ledger. He had shoulder-length blond hair and a scruffy beard. A cigarette with a half-inch-long ash dangled from one corner of his mouth.

"I'm looking for Johnny," Molly said.

He glanced up, blue eyes set in deep sockets beneath shaggy blond brows. He took a drag on the cigarette and smashed it out in the metal ashtray on the desk. He angled the chair toward the door so that he was facing Molly. His T-shirt was red with *I'd Rather Be Hunting* written across his chest in black. "You found him."

"Your wife said it was okay to come on back."

"What can I do for you?" He didn't rise or ask her to sit down. There was no other chair in the tiny makeshift office.

Molly leaned against the door frame. She introduced herself and explained that she was investigating the death of a woman who'd died Sunday night.

"You with the police?"

"The Cherokee Nation," Molly clarified. "I've got some ID." She started rummaging in her purse.

He waved off the suggestion. "That's okay." He grinned, exposing tobacco-stained teeth. "I'll talk to anybody to keep from working on the books. Can't think what you'd want to talk to me about, though."

"The woman who died at the library—her ex-husband claims he was in here about midnight Sunday night."

"The night this woman died?"

"Right. His name's Dell Greer. Do you know him?"

He frowned and shook his head. "Name doesn't ring a

bell." He gazed at Molly for a moment. "The woman who died—is that the one hanged herself?"

"That's what we thought at first, but it turns out she didn't hang herself. She was dead before she was put on the gallows."

His eyes got wide. "Really? And you think this Greer guy's the one who did it?"

"We don't have much evidence on anybody yet. Right now I'm just checking out alibis."

"Gee, this is intriguing. I used to read Hardy Boys books when I was a kid, used to think I'd grow up to be a detective." He looked around the cramped little office. "Life's full of surprises, ain't it? I sure wish I could help you, but I don't know this Greer."

"He's part-Cherokee, thin, about five-ten, stringy black hair. He said he came in Sunday night to buy some Skoal."

He brightened. "Yeah, I do remember him. I didn't have much business after ten o'clock, but a guy like you described did come in, said he was trying to stop smoking. I remember because I keep saying I'm gonna quit, but I never do." He lifted his shoulders in a helpless shrug. "Anyway, he bought three tins of Skoal and something else . . . gum drops, I think. Personally, I can't see how dipping Skoal's gonna help. Tobacco is tobacco, am I right?"

"Yes," Molly agreed, "and with chewing tobacco you have to keep spitting." Molly shuddered. "Disgusting."

He grinned. "There you go. Have to keep a can with you to spit in. Can't see it. I'd be kicking the damned thing over all the time. If I ever do quit, it'll be cold turkey."

"Best way, I guess," Molly said, wanting to get back on track. "Do you remember what time he came in?"

He rubbed his chin through the scraggly beard. "Late. I

was reading a magazine, hadn't had a customer in a while." He raised a questioning eyebrow. "One o'clock, maybe."

"Could it have been earlier or later than that?"

"Sure. Coulda been an hour or so either way. Like I said, I was in the middle of an article on hunting grizzlys, and I went right back to it when he left. Didn't notice the time."

The time period was right for Greer to have been in town when Talia was killed. "Did you notice which way he went when he left the store—toward town or the other way." The Native American Research Library was on the opposite side of town. Greer would have had to take the main street, Muskogee Avenue, and follow the highway past the Cherokee Nation complex to get there.

"No, sorry."

Molly thanked him and turned to go.

"If I think of anything else, where can I reach you?"

She found a card in her purse and handed it to him. She didn't expect to hear from him. The guy had told her all he knew.

She thanked him again and left. Outside, she sat in the Accord for a few minutes, trying to decide what to do next. She wanted to talk to Ina Beaver, but not with Agasuyed present. She started the car. If Ina was still grocery shopping, maybe she could spot the Chevy and catch her when she left the store. There weren't that many grocery stores in Tahlequah. She'd start with the biggest one and work down.

She drove slowly through two store lots and didn't see the Beavers' car. But as she was leaving the second one, the Chevy passed her, Ina at the wheel. She wasn't heading in the direction of Eagle Rock, though. Molly pulled in a couple of cars behind the Chevy and followed Ina through town. Ina turned in at Wal-Mart.

By the time Molly found a parking space, Ina was nowhere in sight. Molly went into the store and looked around. She didn't see Ina.

The wide main aisle had narrower aisles opening off it on both sides. Molly walked along it, checking the side aisles as she passed. She spotted Ina in the home section. She was holding a bath towel up, staring at it, but Molly got the feeling Ina wasn't really seeing the towel. Her mind was somewhere else.

Ina was tired. Molly could tell by the way she seemed to sag into her dress as if she might have slept in it for a week. Or rather worn it for a week. Ina didn't look as if she'd been getting much sleep.

Molly walked up behind Ina and cleared her throat. "Hello, Mrs. Beaver."

Ina jumped and whirled around. Her scoop-necked cotton dress was not flattering. It drew attention to Ina's prominent collarbone and thin neck. Ina refolded the towel and put it back on the shelf. "Hello," she mumbled. She pushed her basket farther down the aisle.

Molly followed. "I went out to Eagle Rock earlier," she said. "I wanted to talk to you."

Ina halted beside a pile of towels on a sale table and picked up a blue one. "You already talked to me."

"We've come up with new evidence in Talia's death."

Ina's only response was to drop the blue towel and pick up a yellow one. She checked the hems, found one corner frayed, and discarded the towel. She rummaged under the pile for another yellow one. There was something about her, the way her narrow shoulders slumped forward that made her seem incredibly sad.

"We recovered one of those threatening notes in Talia's mobile home," Molly said. "The lab found several fingerprints on it." Which was absolutely true, as far as it went.

The shift in Ina's stance was barely perceptible, reminding Molly of an animal alerted by a sudden noise. Ina crushed a towel to her scrawny breast and glanced around, as though searching for somebody to rescue her. Then she looked at Molly reluctantly. "I'm in a hurry. I've got groceries in the car. Why are you bothering me with this?"

"I talked to a boy named Eddie at Eagle Rock this morning. He saw you go to Talia's mobile home Sunday morning after Talia left for church."

It took several moments for her to answer. She dropped the towel she was holding into her basket and started to reach for another yellow one, changed her mind. Her hands were trembling.

"Mrs. Beaver, are you all right?"

She twisted her hands in a tight, wringing motion. Finally, she said, "I'm fine."

"Then you did go to Talia's Sunday?"

After a long hesitation, she nodded. "Yes. I wanted to talk to her. We used to be friends and I—" She glanced into Molly's eyes, then looked away. "I thought we could talk over our differences." She picked up a couple more towels, dropped them in her basket. Then she wheeled it quickly around the corner to the next aisle. She was pretending to examine some plastic drinking glasses when Molly caught up with her.

She looked around at Molly. "If you don't leave me alone," she said, "I'll have to find somebody who can make you."

Molly didn't move. "If you'd rather talk to the Sheriff, that can be arranged."

She didn't threaten to get help again. She didn't say anything. She just gazed at Molly with a kind of trapped expression. Molly would not have been surprised if Ina burst into tears, or made a break for it. But she did neither.

"The boy, Eddie, says you knocked and when Talia didn't answer, you bent down." Something flickered in Ina's eyes. Fear? Molly went on, "You slipped that note under Talia's door, didn't you, Mrs. Beaver?"

She grabbed hold of the push bar on her basket with both hands. Molly braced herself, thinking that Ina might be going to ram the basket into her. Ina seemed agitated enough to do almost anything. But she didn't move the basket—she seemed frozen in place. "You can't prove that," she said grimly. Her knuckles were pale from gripping the bar so tightly.

"Don't be so sure. Fingerprints . . ." Molly let Ina finish the thought.

She bowed her head and swallowed hard.

Molly could see she was upsetting the woman; she definitely had her on the defensive and felt a flicker of guilt. She brushed it aside. "I imagine the Sheriff is planning to call you and your husband and Dell Greer in for fingerprinting."

Ina released her grip on the bar and stared at her rough hands, the jagged nails. "That won't be necessary. I don't want Agasuyed brought into this. I put that note under Talia's door."

"And the other notes?"

She nodded. "Them, too." She let go of the basket, turning her back on it to face Molly squarely. Her work-worn hands gripped each other tightly at her waist. "She was keeping Agasuyed in a constant state of turmoil because she wouldn't leave Eagle Rock," she said with great earnestness, hoping perhaps that Molly would understand. "My husband shouldn't get excited. He isn't well. I was trying to help him."

"Are you saying he knows nothing about the notes?"

"Of course not!"

Molly wasn't sure whether she believed her. Agasuyed could have written the notes and told Ina to deliver them.

"Agasuyed thought his medicine ceremonies would drive her away," Ina went on. "He's been making medicine at dawn and dusk—even at night." Abruptly, she pressed her hands over her mouth and her next words were muffled. "He didn't mean to cause her death. Neither one of us wanted that. Who would have thought she'd kill herself?"

"She didn't," Molly said.

She dropped her hands to stare at Molly. "But the Sheriff said—"

"That was before we got the autopsy report. She was murdered, Mrs. Beaver. Strangled. Before she was put on the gallows."

Ina exhaled in a rush of air and tugged at a strand of her short hair. Finally, she shook her head, as if that could make it not true. "But—who . . . ?" She stammered to a halt as her mind made the connection. "You can't think that I—" She shook her head adamantly.

"The note we found said it was the last warning."

She paled and reached out with one hand to grasp the edge of a shelf for support. Molly stared at the woman's thin arms, the small, rough hands. Ina Beaver could be the one who had attacked Talia and left her bruised and terrified. But did those hands contain enough strength to squeeze the life out of a younger, larger woman?

"I was just trying to scare her into leaving," Ina whimpered. Her dark eyes searched Molly's face. To see if the truth was getting through to Molly? Or to see if Molly was buying her lies?

"Did you attack Talia, too?"

Her eyes darted to one side. "I didn't hurt her much. I only hit her once, to scare her." She covered her face with her hands and made a little moaning sound. Dropping her hands, she said, "She stumbled and I could have hit her again without her seeing me. But I didn't. Please don't tell my husband. I hit Talia and sent those notes, but I could never kill anybody. I can't even kill a squirrel with Agasuyed's shotgun." Tears gathered in her eyes. "You have to believe me."

"It doesn't matter much what I believe, Mrs. Beaver. The Sheriff will want to talk to you."

"But we were at home Sunday night. We've already told the Sheriff that."

Molly gripped the strap of her bag, which was slung over her shoulder. "If I were you, Mrs. Beaver, I'd go straight to the Sheriff's office and tell him everything you've told me. It'll be worse if he has to come out to Eagle Rock and pick you up."

With that, Molly walked away, leaving Ina Beaver cowering like a whipped dog in the aisle between the drinking glasses and the pots and pans. The woman was pathetic, and Molly felt like a bully. But Ina Beaver could well have been involved in Talia Wind's murder, at least as an accomplice to her husband.

She was almost certain Ina would go to the Sheriff. Ina didn't want him to talk to Agasuyed again. Ina was bent on protecting her husband. Because he wasn't well, Ina said. Maybe. But suppose she knew—or feared—that her husband was the killer. If so, she would be afraid of what Agasuyed might reveal if the Sheriff talked to him again.

Molly thought about everything she knew. Agasuyed had been making medicine to drive Talia away from Eagle Rock. He'd been doing ceremonies day and night, according to Ina. Even though Talia Wind had made medicine in the middle of the night, it was unusual to perform medicine ceremonies at night. Molly recalled the way Ina's hand had gone to her mouth when she'd said that, as if she'd let something she hadn't intended slip out.

According to the Beavers, they'd been home together all Sunday evening and night. But Ina would lie for her husband. Had Agasuyed left the house Sunday night, telling Ina he was going to make medicine?

If so, Ina would have no way of knowing for sure that's what he'd done. He could have gone in search of Talia—and found her.

Ina was definitely scared. She might only be frightened for herself, wondering if the Sheriff would try to turn her admission about writing the notes into a murder charge. But Molly had the feeling that Ina was more concerned with protecting Agasuyed than herself.

Sitting in the car, Molly closed her eyes and saw Talia Wind's swollen, purple, dead face. The image was burned into her mind like the afterimage of a flash.

Both Agasuyed Beaver and Dell Greer were strong enough to have strangled the life from Talia. But was Ina?

She opened her eyes, started the engine and drove out of the Wal-Mart lot, still thinking about Ina. It was hard to imagine Ina strangling Talia. It was easier to see Agasuyed or Greer in that role. But where was the evidence?

Frustrated, Molly glanced down at the odometer. The Accord had seventy-two thousand miles on it, but that wasn't bad for an eleven-year-old car. She liked the way it handled.

She wondered why Tim Dowell hadn't gotten back to her about the repairs on her Civic. Maybe the news was even worse than he'd first thought and he was putting off telling her.

She glanced at her watch. It was close enough to noon to have lunch, so she drove back through town and stopped at Braum's for a steak sandwich and coffee. She sat at a booth next to the window. While she ate and watched the traffic, she tried to work out where she should go next with the murder investigation. Later that afternoon, she'd check in with Sheriff Hobart, see if Ina took her advice and went in to make a statement.

At some point, she would have to give the Sheriff the name of Talia's lover. But Molly hoped to talk to Josh Rollins first. She wished she could trust Hobart to accept her as a full partner in the investigation, but her experience with the Sheriff didn't engender that much trust. Hobart's grudging attitude forced her to conduct her own investigation, so she didn't feel obligated to let him in on everything she knew immediately.

He'd be hopping mad if he found out she'd known about Rollins's place in Talia's life long before she told him. But he'd get over it.

She finished the steak sandwich and ordered a dip of pecans, praline, and cream ice cream and a coffee refill.

Josh Rollins's restaurant north of town was called the Silver Flame Steakhouse. It didn't open until one, which gave

Molly an hour to figure out what she was going to say to the man.

She hoped to question Rollins's wife, Belinda, too. The thought made Molly squirm. From that look the wife had thrown Talia at the wild onion breakfast, Belinda knew that Talia was interested in her husband, though she might not know that her husband was equally attracted to Talia.

Either way, it gave Belinda Rollins a motive to want Talia out of her husband's life for good. The woman hated Talia, probably saw her as a threat to her marriage. A not uncommon motive for murder. But how could she have known where Talia would be Sunday night?

You never fail in anything,
for so it was ordained of you.

13

Neither Josh nor Belinda Rollins was at the restaurant when Molly got there shortly after one o'clock. The well-groomed, middle-aged hostess said they were out of town for the day. She wouldn't give Molly their home address or phone number. Molly had already checked the phone book and hadn't found them listed.

The hostess seemed to assume that Molly was there to apply for a job and Molly didn't correct her. She merely thanked the woman, but didn't leave her name. She preferred that the Rollinses not be forewarned she wanted to talk to them.

For the time being, her investigation was stymied.

Deciding reluctantly to check in with the Sheriff and get it over with, she drove to the courthouse. The Sheriff's Department, City Hall, and the Tahlequah Police Department were housed in a long, flat-topped, three-story structure faced with big, pebbly slabs of tan concrete. Molly parked at one end of the building near an entrance that took her directly to the second-floor foyer and, from there, to the Sheriff's offices.

Finding no one at the reception desk, she walked back to the Sheriff's office. The open door revealed pine-paneled walls, worn brown indoor-outdoor carpeting, and two walls adorned with maps of Oklahoma and Cherokee County. Old metal shelving crammed with reports and files hid the other two walls. The county commissioners weren't wasting any of the taxpayers' money on decorations.

Hobart sat at a big old metal desk whose top was covered with more stacked papers and file folders plus a couple of telephone directories. His back to the door, he pounded the keys of an ancient manual typewriter which rested on a shelf that pulled out of one side of the desk. Light from naked fluorescent ceiling tubes hit the top of Hobart's head, exposing shiny pink scalp between strands of thinning white hair.

He bent closer to the sheet of paper in the typewriter, muttered an oath, back-spaced, and typed over a word. He added another line, then gave a satisfied grunt and pulled the paper from the platen.

Molly was about to announce herself when Hobart sensed her presence and spun around in his swivel chair.

"Shit!" he yelped in surprise. "Where'd you come from? Becky shoulda told me you were here."

Presumably Becky was the absent receptionist. "Nobody's in the outer office," Molly said, "so I came on back."

"Oh, yeah, I forgot. She's gone to lunch."

"Do you have a couple of minutes?"

"I guess," he said grudgingly, "but that's about all I've got."

Molly moved a cardboard box from a chair and sat down. "Did Ina Beaver come to see you?"

He nodded. "I just finished typing her statement." He dropped the paper on top of a stack of folders and leaned back in his chair. "She wanted to file a complaint against you, but I talked her out of it. Don't ask me why."

"A complaint! You're kidding."

"No. She said you cornered her at Wal-Mart, forced her to talk to you, then ordered her to come here."

"I did not order her! I suggested that she tell you what she told me—which she did of her own free will, by the way. No force was necessary."

She might as well have been talking to the wall. "Lying and bullying witnesses is not the way we do business around here, Molly."

"I did not bully her—wait a minute," she stammered, "what lies?"

"She said," he told her angrily, "that you told her we found her fingerprints on that note we took from Talia Wind's trailer."

Molly came out of her chair. "That's not true. I said the lab had found fingerprints on the note. She jumped to her own conclusions."

"Just like you knew she would," he countered.

"I was trying to help, Sheriff."

He rose, planted his hands on the edge of the desk, and leaned forward. His face was turning red. "I know it's hard for you to imagine," he said, his voice rising, "but we managed to solve a crime or two around here before the Cherokee Nation, in its infinite wisdom, decided to inflict you on us."

"Nobody's saying you didn't." Molly's voice had risen, too. She tamped it down a notch. "Look, I know you're short-handed. You need another investigator, whether you'll admit it or not."

"What I do not need is a hotshot running loose, conducting her own secret investigation."

"It's no secret!" she snapped. "And if you'd cooperate, I wouldn't have to do it by myself."

"Cooperation is a two-way street."

"Granted!"

They stared at each other, having reached a stalemate. Finally, Molly pointed at the statement Hobart had just finished typing. "May I look at that?"

Hobart glared at her. She glared back. "I want to see if her stories jibe."

"Oh, hell," he grumbled as he snatched up the report and thrust it at her. "Go ahead."

"Thank you," she said sweetly.

He stood and watched her. She read the statement quickly and handed it back to him. "Same story she told me."

He tossed the statement on his desk. "If I'd had first shot at her, no telling what I'd have got out of her."

"Look—" Molly stopped herself. She wanted to tell him that he would've gotten zip if Molly hadn't run interference. Hobart would bite his tongue off before he would admit that Molly was actually contributing to the investigation. No point in adding to the strain between them. "I checked that convenience store where Dell Greer said he went Sunday night. He was there around midnight. He could easily have gone to the library from there and murdered Talia."

He forced a tight little smile. "Thanks for pointing that out."

Molly chose to ignore the juvenile sarcasm. "Trouble is,

the way those places at Eagle Rock are situated, almost any of the residents could have come to town Sunday night without the neighbors knowing it." She might have told him about Josh Rollins, too, if he'd shown the slightest inkling that he would work with her.

"Hot damn, you've been busy, a regular Nancy Drew."

"Listen here—"

"No, you listen, Miss Major Crimes Investigator." His voice shook with anger. "I'm the Sheriff. I'm charged with the responsibility of investigating, to the best of my ability, the crimes in Cherokee County when they occur outside the jurisdiction of another law enforcement agency. I can't do that if you keep getting to these people ahead of me."

"And I can't do my job if you keep freezing me out! Correction. It's harder to do my job, but I *will* do it. Without your cooperation—you've made it clear I won't be getting that. If you change your mind, let me know. Good afternoon, Sheriff."

Molly stormed out of the office.

She'd cooled down several degrees by the time she got to her office. D.J. had left a message on the answering machine, asking her if she wanted to have dinner before he went to work. She called him back to tell him she was meeting her father for dinner.

"That's great, sweetheart," he said enthusiastically.

She opened a desk drawer and rummaged around for a Snickers bar. Only a piece of a bar remained in her comfort food stash. She needed to restock. She peeled the wrapping off the half-eaten bar. "I hope it goes okay," she said. "I'll just be glad when it's over. I'm so nervous thinking about it I could jump out of my skin."

"This is your father, Molly. I don't care what happened in the past, he loves you. And I'll bet you're going to find he had what seemed to him good reasons for staying away from you for so long." He paused and when he spoke again an earnest note had crept into his voice. "Molly, I can tell you from personal experience that sometimes circumstances or other people keep a man from doing what he needs and wants to do for his kid."

So that was it. D.J. had been defending her father because he identified with him. His ex-wife was remarried and living in Colorado with her new husband and D.J.'s daughter, Courtney. D.J. only saw Courtney twice a year, and the guilt ate at him.

"Oh, D.J.," Molly said, "you can't compare your situation to my father's."

There was a pause and an indrawn breath. "Sometimes I really hate Gloria for taking her so far away," he said finally.

Never had Molly wanted so much to touch him, to put her arms around him. "I know, honey, but she has custody and you have no control over where she lives. Don't beat up on yourself."

"My head knows you're right, but it's hard."

She laughed shakily. "Tell me about it."

"What really gets to me is that Gloria's husband is there, day in and day out. He's the one who drives Courtney to school and goes to see her play softball. He's going to be there when she goes on her first date and when she graduates from high school. She'll either resent me or forget all about me."

"I don't think so. Every child wants a relationship with

both parents. If Courtney seems not to now, she will when she's grown."

"Hey, aren't you the woman who told me she wished her father had stayed gone?"

His words hit home. Face it, Molly, she told herself. "So I lied." She smiled. "I'm just scared, D.J. And it doesn't mean I still don't resent his desertion, probably always will."

"It'll be okay, sugar."

"I needed that. It hasn't been my best day. I had a run-in with your boss."

"What happened?"

She told him, adding, "I guess I'm out of the loop on this one, not that I was ever in."

"Hang in, sweetheart. Claude won't be Sheriff much longer. And call me when you get home, after you've seen your father. Have the dispatcher beep me if I'm out."

Molly went home to change before dinner. She tried on several outfits, from jeans and a cotton shirt to a ruffled silk dress her grandmother had given her, and finally settled on something in between—a plaid skirt and yellow cotton sweater. She even put on pantyhose and high-heeled pumps, then discarded the pumps as too dressy and settled for beige flats with one-inch stacked heels.

She brushed her long, black hair and left it loose, adding a yellow headband to keep it in place.

She arrived at The Shack at six forty-five and took a corner booth. She sat facing the front of the café so she would see him when he came in. Would he recognize her—or she, him?

A waitress brought her a glass of water and a menu. Molly told her she was meeting someone and asked for a cup of coffee while she waited. Only three other booths and a table were occupied. It was a slow night.

By seven, she'd drunk two cups of coffee and turned down a third. By ten after seven, she'd cleaned out her purse and drunk two glasses of water and had to go to the rest room.

When she came out of the rest room, she scanned the café. The couple at the table had left. Nobody new had come in. At seven-twenty, she phoned her grandmother.

"Have you heard from my father?"

"Not today. Didn't you meet him for dinner?"

"I'm at the café now. He hasn't shown up."

"Something must have happened to make him late. He was thrilled when I told him you'd meet him for dinner."

"I'll wait another ten minutes, Grandmother, and then I'm out of here."

By seven-thirty, two men had entered the café separately. One was blond, the other in his twenties. Neither of them could possibly be Rob Bearpaw.

Seething with a mixture of anger and disappointment, Molly went to the counter to pay for her coffee. The waitress was on the phone. She looked over at Molly. "Aren't you Molly Bearpaw?" Molly nodded and the waitress dangled the receiver in front of her. "This is for you."

Molly reached for the phone. Taut nerves made her hand shake. It must be her father, calling to tell her why he hadn't come. She took a deep breath and put the receiver to her ear. "Hello."

"Molly?" It was D.J.

"D.J., what—"

"Can you come to the courthouse?"

"What—? *Now*, you mean?"

"Now, yes. Your father's here."

"At the Sheriff's office? What's he doing there?"

"He's in custody, Molly."

"In—" Words failed her. She felt a nerve beside her eye start to twitch. She closed her eyes for a moment, then asked, "What's he done?"

"Just come. I'll explain everything when you get here."

"What are you doing there now? Your shift doesn't start till midnight."

"Brock and I came on at six. Two deputies called in sick. We got a flu bug going around."

"Does my father know you called me?"

"He asked me to. That's about all he's talked about, missing his dinner date with you."

"Okay, D.J. I'm on the way."

Molly hung up and rushed from the restaurant. On the drive to the courthouse, she forced her hands to relax on the wheel and tried to get a grip on the anxiety that had attacked her as she talked to D.J.

What had her father done? Hurt somebody? Broken into a house? She realized that she had no idea whether her father was capable of either of those things. She didn't know him, but she fiercely resented being summoned to the county jail because he'd been arrested.

All she'd wanted was to meet the man, have dinner, see if there was anything there to build a relationship on. Maybe plan to see him again. Take it slow and easy. Instead, he'd gotten himself arrested.

It wasn't her problem, dammit.

Her vision had grown fuzzy and she realized that tears had come to her eyes. She blinked them away. Okay, she wasn't going to panic. Not until she knew what he'd done. Maybe it was something minor.

And who else could he call? Eva didn't need this aggravation. Molly could be grateful for one thing. He'd asked for her rather than her grandmother.

Ha! Now you are brought down.
There shall be left but a trace upon the ground where you have been.

14

When she reached the building on West Delaware Street, D.J. came to meet her in the second floor's brick-floored foyer. He hugged her, then held her away from him, searching her eyes with concern. "You okay?"

She reached out for another hug, returning the pressure of his arms with hers. "I'm fine," she mumbled against his shoulder.

Then she followed him through the door and down the long hall. The deputy manning the desk watched them curiously from the corner of his eye. His name was Bill something; he was a twenty-year veteran of the department. The desk telephone rang and D.J. hesitated where the hallway turned left. Bill picked up the phone, said hello, held up a hand indicating that D.J. should wait and then listened for a few minutes. He looked at D.J. "Brock's on the line, Kennedy. The stolen car's a new Mercedes sedan. Baby blue. Eighty thousand dollars' worth. Wants to know if you want him to file the report right away."

"Tell him to patrol the area first," D.J. said, "then come back and file."

Bill relayed the message and hung up. "Sheeze. Didn't the last census say Cherokee County was the poorest county in the state?" He shook his head. "Who has that kind of money for a car?"

Both questions seemed to be rhetorical. D.J. took Molly's arm and led her back to the small, open area containing the book-in desk. Nobody was there, and the door leading to the cells was closed.

"Where is he?" she asked.

"We put him in one of the offices temporarily."

At least she wouldn't have to talk to him in a cell. The county jail cells were depressingly grim and claustrophobic, barely big enough for a toilet and an iron cot, with concrete block walls painted tan. Prisoners were issued a mattress and blanket when they were booked in. If they were lucky, they got one of the cells with a narrow, barred window.

"I want to explain a few things before you talk to your dad." He pulled a chair out from the booking desk for her.

She hesitated momentarily, then sat down. "Okay," she said, though she was thinking, My father's under arrest. No explanation can change that.

He unlocked the door leading into the glassed-off end of the room where prisoners who had visitors were brought on Wednesday afternoon, the one day a week they were allowed visitors. The visitors stayed on the outside of the glass and talked to the prisoners through a speaker.

Molly glanced over the signs taped to the wall. One, put up

after a couple of prisoners had decided that eating crushed glass was the fastest way out of jail, said: "Any prisoner who breaks a lightbulb in the jail will be guilty of a felony and will have to either post bond of $1,000 or pay a fine of $100." Another sign listed jail rules: "All locks locked at all times. No tobacco products in jail. Prisoners will be thoroughly searched before being jailed. No prisoner shall be permitted to leave jail and return to visit other prisoners for six months. Visits limited to fifteen minutes."

D.J. dragged a chair through the door and placed it beside the book-in desk, then locked the door again.

"I talked to Claude," D.J. said, sitting down. "He told me to charge your dad with breaking and entering and hold him overnight. Claude will question him tomorrow and decide whether to charge him with anything more—um, more serious."

Molly gazed at D.J. as he talked, thinking that she wanted to flee. She had been worried about what she'd say to her father at dinner, but this was a hundred times worse. "You caught him breaking into a house—when he was supposed to be meeting me? I can't believe this."

"Not a house."

Distractedly, she tucked a stray strand of hair under her headband, then curled her fingers around the arms of her chair. "Wherever. The charge is the same. Did he have stolen property in his possession?"

"No." He placed his hand over hers. "It's kind of complicated."

Molly grasped the chair's metal arms tighter. "If he thinks, because of my job, that I have some influence with the Sheriff, we've got news for him, don't we?" She pulled her hand from beneath D.J.'s and sat back in the chair. "In fact, Hobart's probably getting a kick out of locking up my father." She folded her arms over her chest. "Give me all the gory details, D.J." She was struck by another thought. "Oh, Lord, he didn't hurt somebody, did he?"

"Nobody's been hurt, and he didn't steal anything, either— never intended to."

"That's his story?"

"I believe him, Molly. He's no thief. He's just a guy who's down on his luck. He needed a place to bed down and wash up. Maybe he used the stove to heat food a few times, but he cleaned up after himself, left everything as he'd found it. There were several items he could have taken and sold on the street, but he didn't."

"Wait a minute. What do you mean a place to bed down? Was this place vacant at night?"

"Yes."

"Oh, great, a business."

"Sort of. It's the Native American Research Library."

Molly let the implications of that work their way through her brain filters before the worst ramification flashed into her mind, as though lighted in neon.

"Oh, my God. He's been staying in the library at night?"

D.J. nodded.

"How did he get in?"

"He removed one of those big stones near the ground and entered the basement." Molly remembered the mortar dust she'd stepped in down there near the west wall. That was where her father had been getting in. If she'd looked closer at that wall when she was there, the loose stone would have been cemented into place and all this could have been avoided. "In the morning," D.J. was saying, "when he left, he pulled the stone back into place, took his belongings in his duffel with him. A friend of his is letting him use an old pickup. He parked it on a little-traveled side road near the library at night. During the day he'd park it somewhere in town. Spent a lot of time at the public library, he says."

She shook her head. "I'm getting a real bad feeling here. You mentioned that Claude is considering more serious charges."

"He'll have to have more evidence than we've got now."

"Don't try to sugarcoat it for me, D.J. Was my father in the library the night Talia was murdered?"

He reached for her hand again and squeezed. "He says he wasn't, sweetheart. He says he was visiting an old friend in town, the same one who's letting him use the pickup. He was there until very late and when he went to the library and started to go in, he heard what sounded like chanting coming from inside. So he grabbed his duffel and left, bedded down in an old abandoned garage behind a store on the main street. That wasn't a break-in—the garage wasn't locked."

Molly clasped her hands tightly in her lap and bowed her head. "Of course there's nobody who can back up his story."

He shook his head. "Huh-uh. He took pains not to be seen."

"How'd he get caught at the library?"

"Alice Mundy went back to the library about six forty-five this evening for something she'd meant to take home with her. She unlocked the front door and turned on some lights. He was standing at the bottom of the stairs, bare-chested. He'd been cleaning up before going to meet you. He tried to duck out of sight, but she saw him."

"Must have scared her spitless."

"Yeah. What with all the ghost stories, she was already

edgy about going in alone. She ran back to her car, which was parked out front, locked herself in, and called us from her cell phone. I happened to take the call. I got there in time to catch him climbing out of the basement with his duffel."

Molly fought an impulse to throw herself into D.J.'s arms again and weep. "Why didn't he tell somebody he had no money to rent a room? There are agencies who would help him. Even Eva would probably have let him stay with her for a few days. My God, he could have thrown a sleeping bag on my floor." She might not have liked it, but she wouldn't have turned him away to live on the streets.

"Try to put yourself in his shoes, Molly."

She chewed her bottom lip to keep from crying. "That's a tough one." She didn't *know* her father, so how could she know what he was feeling or thinking?

"He's probably ashamed," D.J. went on. "He was recently approved for Social Security disability, but his first check didn't come until today. He's got a post office box in town. I guess he figured he'd have a place anyday, and nobody would have to know he was temporarily homeless." He smiled wryly. "It almost worked out for him, too. Even the owner of the pickup didn't know he was homeless."

"How long has he been in town?"

"Almost three weeks. He hitched a ride from some place in Nebraska. He worked there for years—till he couldn't hold down a job anymore."

Molly didn't ask what was wrong with her father, why he could no longer work. What if he had come home to die? That's what animals did, wasn't it—crawl back home to die? Maybe it was a basic human instinct, too.

She covered her face with both hands, dragged in some air. It was just too much to cope with all at once.

"He asked if I'd let him talk to you in one of the offices," D.J. said. "He didn't want you to see him for the first time, after twenty-five years, behind bars."

Molly dropped her hands. This was the moment she had been dreading. More than anything right then, she wanted to run out of that room, out of the courthouse and drive to her apartment. She wanted to crawl into bed, with Homer curled up on the floor beside her, and pull the covers over her head.

She recognized the impulse as childish—if they can't see you, the monsters won't get you.

D.J. watched her closely. He knew her well enough to guess what she was thinking and feeling by her body language.

He touched her cheek. "It'll be okay. You ready?"

Ready to see her father in custody? No.

Molly pushed herself out of the chair, smoothed back her hair. "Ready as I'll ever be."

The deputy at the reception desk watched them as they turned the corner headed for the offices. D.J. unlocked the outer door to the reception room. A single pink carnation in a glass vase graced one file cabinet and a stuffed rabbit rested atop another. The receptionist's attempt to add a few homey touches. It didn't work for Molly.

D.J. led the way to an office that was smaller than the Sheriff's but with the same pine-paneled walls. There were a desk occupied by a computer and printer, a table with boxes of files stacked at one end, and more metal shelves on one wall. The space over the desk was covered by a large map of Oklahoma, like the one in the Sheriff's office. A huge calendar compliments of a local funeral home hung on another wall.

Finally, Molly looked at the man seated at the table facing the door. He was thin, barrel-chested, with high cheekbones and hollow cheeks. Deep lines fanned out from the corners of his dark eyes and formed parentheses from his nose to the corners of his mouth. His skin had gone a little slack with the years. A pack of filtered cigarettes and a lighter lay on the table next to an ashtray containing several stubs.

His eyes slid past D.J. and fixed on Molly. He came to his feet slowly, "Molly?"

"I'll leave you two alone," D.J. said. He pulled the desk chair over to the table for Molly and touched her shoulder lightly. "I'll be right outside if you need me." He left, closing the door behind him.

"Ah, Miss Molly." The stranger stared at her as if intent on memorizing her face. "You look so much like your mother."

What was the happiest thing that happened to you today, Miss Molly?

"Do I? I can't remember what she looked like, but I never thought the picture Grandmother has in her living room looked much like me."

He had on jeans that had been laundered so many times they were almost white and a blue chambray shirt with a neat patch on one sleeve. He was clean, but he needed a haircut.

"She was pretty, like you," he said.

He was about five-ten, with big, rough hands. There was something about the set of his mouth and his eyes that touched a chord in Molly's memory.

She was still standing where D.J. had left her and beginning to feel extremely awkward.

"Sit down, sit down," he said.

She took the chair across the table from him. He waited for her to sit before he did. He tapped a cigarette out of the package and lit it. The lighter was red plastic. When the flame went out, he looked at Molly, squinting as he took a drag and blew the smoke toward the ceiling.

She sat straight in the chair, hands clasped in her lap, like a child called to the principal's office. "Grandmother says you're not well."

He nodded. "It's my lungs. Emphysema. I traveled with a wheat harvest crew for twenty years, and worked at a grain elevator in Nebraska the rest of the year. It took its toll. I got a little spray thing I carry with me that helps. The way the doctor explained it, with emphysema your lungs lose their elasticity. Usually you can breathe in okay, it's the breathing out that's hard. Sitting here like this, I don't notice it so much. But I walk half a block, and I can't get my breath. Have to stop and rest for a while, then I can walk another half block. That's on my good days."

She eyed the cigarette which he held between thumb and index finger. "I can't believe smoking is helping."

"No." He took another drag and winced as if it were painful. "The doctor in Nebraska and the one at the Indian hospital here both told me I have to quit."

She lifted a brow. "They won't let you smoke in jail."

He reached for the ashtray and stubbed out the cigarette. "I know." He sat back in his chair, arms extended on the table, exposing bony wrists that looked as if they should be attached to smaller hands. "I was planning to quit, anyway, soon as I got into my own place."

"You didn't have to break into the library," Molly said. "You should have asked somebody for help."

He lifted his shoulders. "Yeah. But I remembered how my friends and I used to get into the old jail after they stopped using it, and I checked and that stone was still loose." A grin flickered and was gone, stirring another long-buried memory. "It seemed like a good idea at the time. Turned out to be the worst place I could've picked."

Molly nodded, waited for him to go on.

"I slept in the basement, used the bathroom, heated up a can of soup or something, and left early the next morning."

"Where did you go then?"

"A friend of mine's letting me use his pickup till I get on my feet. Bill Spring. He used to come by the house in Park Hill. You remember him?"

"No, but I know who he is. I've seen him around town."

"Bill doesn't know where I was spending the nights, or he'd have insisted I stay with him." He fiddled with the lighter. "I don't think his wife wanted me around all that much. When I left the old jail, I'd go to the doughnut shop for breakfast, then park somewhere. Couldn't afford to burn up much gas. Sometimes I went to the public library and read." He tapped the lighter with one finger. "Every time I passed Cherokee Square, where Eva said you worked, I was hoping to catch a glimpse of you. Never happened."

"So you didn't tell anybody you were homeless."

He shook his head. "I was ashamed. Besides, I knew I'd be getting a check any day." He gave her an odd little half-smile. "Funny thing is, my first check came today. I was going to look for a place to rent tomorrow. A day or two earlier, and I'd have been home free." He gestured vaguely around the room. "I'm sorry—about all this. I was looking forward to our dinner."

Her mouth felt dry. "Me, too," she said. It seemed to be what he wanted to hear.

He leaned forward. "I wish you didn't have to come to a place like this, but I had to talk to you." He hesitated, waiting for a response from her.

"I've been in places like this before," she said.

"I keep forgetting. You're some kind of investigator for the Cherokee Nation. I've spent a lot of time imagining how you'd grown up, what you were doing, but I never imagined that."

What was she supposed to say now? Gee, Dad, thanks for thinking about me? How hard was it to pick up the phone and ask? She kept quiet.

"I've wanted to call you so many times," he said, as if reading her thoughts.

She couldn't let that pass. "Why didn't you? I hear they have phones in Nebraska."

He shrugged and laced his fingers together on the tabletop. His nails were uneven, the skin beneath them bluish. Staring down at his hands, he said, "I felt like I gave up the right to a relationship with you when I listened to—when I left."

When he listened to what, who? "A phone call once in a while isn't exactly a relationship. Did you think I didn't want to hear from you?"

He lifted his head. There was pain in his eyes. "I want to explain, Molly, but I don't want to cause any problems with Eva . . ."

Molly bristled. "Don't you dare criticize Grandmother," she flared. "She's a saint in my book! She loved me, reared me, helped me go to college. She's *the* most important person in my life, ever."

He passed a hand across his face, as if to sweep away a shadow. "I know she is, and that's why I went along with what she wanted."

Molly stiffened. "What does that mean?"

"When I found out your mother was dead, I called Eva. I knew I couldn't have you with me all the time, but I wanted to be able to phone you, to come see you when I could. Eva said no. She had a real strong opinion about it. Said I should come home and take care of you myself or stay out of the picture completely." His voice trembled. "I couldn't come home, Molly, not then."

Molly stared at him. "Are you saying Grandmother told you not to call, not to come to see me?"

He nodded. "After that, when I called anyway, she hung up on me. Please don't take this as a criticism, either. She was thinking of you, Molly. She thought it would be easier for you to—well, accept the situation, if I made no contact. That's all she asked of me and I was pretty much of an emotional wreck at the time, so I finally accepted that that's the way it had to be. I'd joined AA and was off booze, but I was filled with guilt about leaving you and about Josie."

Which he damn well should have been, Molly thought. She had gripped the edge of the table with one hand, and he reached toward her reflexively, then drew his hand back and tapped out another cigarette. He lit it, sucked on it.

"I thought I was saving both of us—Josie and me—when I left. I know the shooting went down as a suicide, but Eva said it was accidental." He looked at her through a plume of smoke.

"It was no accident," she said flatly.

He tapped an ash into the ashtray. "I never thought she'd kill herself."

She leaned back in her chair, folding her arms across her chest. "How could you think leaving Mama would save her?" Suddenly, she wanted to hit him, to wipe that pleading look off his face. She pushed back her chair. "You know what, I don't think I can continue this right now . . ."

He half-rose from his chair, taking quick, shallow breaths. "Molly, hear me out. *Please.*"

She stopped, folded her arms again. She felt suddenly cold and wished she had a sweater. Finally, she sat back down.

He took several more shallow breaths, then said, "I loved your mother. I truly did. But the marriage was destroying us, Molly."

Molly stared at the wall behind him.

"I know you probably can't remember how it was, but we drank all the time. I lost track of the times I tried to go on the wagon. Josie wouldn't even try, said she didn't have a problem. And she'd keep wheedling until she talked me into taking her to this bar where we hung out. I could never say no to that woman for long. We'd get there and I'd end up ordering a drink."

"That's bull! Nobody could make that decision for you. It was your choice. Just like it was your choice not to contact me until now."

He raised a hand. "I know it sounds like I'm blaming Josie for my drinking, but I'm not. I haven't for a long time. It wasn't hard for her to get me to go to the bar with her. I was weak. Truth is, I wanted to drink again, and so I told myself it wasn't my fault, played the blame game. We were what they call nowadays co-dependent—we enabled each other to keep drinking." He shook his head. "I sound like a durned psychologist, don't I? We talk like that in AA. Anyway, finally, about the hundredth time I decided to stop, it just hit me that I could never make it stick as long as Josie and I were together. I didn't have the backbone. I meant to come back, Molly, as soon as I knew I was strong enough to stay sober. I thought I'd be able to help Josie then." He bowed his head, covered his face with his hands. When he looked up, there were tears in his eyes. "I—I just waited too long."

"You sure did." Her tone gave no quarter.

He swiped his shirtsleeve across his eyes, bowed his head again. The silence lengthened. Molly looked away from him, gazed out a window at a few inches of an oak branch outlined against a deepening gray sky. It had been the kind of early May day that was neither true spring nor summer, but something in between, something tentative and poised somehow, and now it was slipping peacefully into night.

"When I was little," she said quietly, "I used to pray every night that you'd come back."

"I'm sorry," he mumbled miserably.

"By the time I was in my teens, I hated you." She glanced at him. He sat still with bowed head. She looked away. "Later, I convinced myself you were dead. That was easier than thinking you didn't give a damn about me."

He spoke, drawing her eyes back to him. "I never stopped loving you. I thought about you all the time."

She shrugged. She wasn't even angry anymore, she just felt depressed.

Finally, he said, "This trouble I'm in—I don't want you involved in it."

"I'm already involved. I'm investigating the murder of Talia Wind."

"I didn't kill her, Molly. I never even saw her."

"But you were there that night, at the library, weren't you?"

He stubbed out his cigarette. "I didn't go in. I started to, but then I heard noises inside, so I left, found another place to sleep that night."

"What time did you go there?"

He squared up the cigarette package with the edge of the table. "Must've been after midnight. I know it was late because it was close to midnight when I left Bill's house. His wife was out of town, so he got some beer and pretzels and invited a couple of other guys over and we played cards. I drank Coke."

"And then you went to the library? What time was that?"

"Like I said, it was maybe five minutes past midnight when I parked the pickup out of sight on an old side road. I walked about a quarter-mile to the library. Had to stop and get my breath a few times, so it took maybe ten or fifteen minutes."

"Then what?"

"I pushed back the shrubs with both hands and crawled up to that big stone, the one I could pull out far enough to crawl in. Grabbed hold of it, but then I heard sounds coming from inside. It sounded like chanting. I couldn't hear it real good, but I know it was somebody talking, and I don't think it was English."

Talia had performed a medicine ceremony. The incantation would not have been in English.

"Did it sound like Cherokee?"

"Could've been. I'm not sure. I couldn't hear that well. Those old stones are good insulators."

"What did you do then?"

"Got out of there fast. Went back to the pickup with my duffel. Drove to town."

"You didn't go around and look in a basement window?"

He shook his head. "I was too spooked. Scared whoever was inside would see me and call the cops."

Molly studied him. "Tell me something. Do you have an arrest record?"

His expression changed. "A couple of old DUIs from when I was with your mother. Nothing else." He reached for a cigarette, shook his head, and pushed the package away from him. "Except for this." He met her steady gaze, but she could tell it was an effort for him not to look away.

"Maybe that'll help," Molly said, "but with the Sheriff, you never know." No point in telling him that being her father might make it even worse for him.

"Why would I kill that woman, Molly? I didn't know her. Never saw her. Never even heard of her till after she was dead. Don't they have to have a motive to charge me with murder? What motive could I have?"

The answer seemed elementary to Molly. "They could try to prove it didn't happen like you said, that you broke into the library and she caught you—or you looked in a basement window and she saw you. So you shut her up."

He stared at her. "You think I'd kill somebody to keep it quiet I was sleeping in the library?"

She wanted to ask him how she was supposed to know what he'd do, but said instead, "I'm just telling you what the Sheriff might be thinking."

The muscles in his face tightened. "It happened exactly like I said. That's the truth and they can't prove anything else."

"Well, they're going to charge you with breaking and entering for sure. You need a lawyer."

"I'm gonna ask for a public defender."

The district judge had a roster of all the lawyers in the county. They assigned the PD cases alphabetically. Maybe he'd get somebody who'd do a good job for him. If Molly had a choice, she'd want Felix Benson, Moira's old boss. But she wouldn't have a choice.

"I'll find out who's assigned and talk to him or her."

"I told you, I don't want you involved in this."

"And I told you I already am."

He took a breath that started him coughing. It was a deep, hacking cough. "Sorry," he said when he could talk. "This cough keeps hanging on. Doc says chronic bronchitis is a side effect of emphysema."

Sleeping on a cold concrete floor hadn't helped much, either, Molly thought. Or smoking one cigarette after another. "Where's your inhaler?"

"The deputy at the desk took it."

She pushed back her chair. "I'll tell him you need it. Then I'm going home. I'll check with you later."

He rose slowly to his feet, bracing himself with his hands on the table. "Thanks for coming, Molly."

She went to the door, hesitated and turned back. "One more question. Did you ever touch the computers in the library?"

"Computers?" he said quizzically. "No. I don't know a thing about computers."

"The nights you slept there, did you hear things—strange noises?"

He looked blank. "Nope, but once I'm asleep it can take an explosion to wake me up. Why?"

"It's not important," Molly said and left.

Stanley Brock and D.J. were leaning against the desk, talking to Bill when she came out into the hall.

Bill pulled out a drawer and extracted a big key ring from which a dozen or so keys dangled. "I'd better go put him in a cell."

"He needs his inhaler," Molly said.

Bill glanced at D.J. "We aren't supposed to let 'em take anything into the cells with 'em."

Until that moment, Molly hadn't realized how close to the edge she was. She turned on the deputy. "If he has to go to the emergency room," she flared, "because you denied him his inhaler, I'll see you in court!"

Bill stepped back, startled by her outburst.

"Give him the inhaler," D.J. said.

Bill pulled out another drawer, found the inhaler and left. The new deputy, Stanley Brock, looked at her curiously, then ducked his head. He was about five-nine, stocky, with a square face and military-style crew cut.

"Tough talking to him, huh?" D.J. asked her.

Molly didn't bother responding. The answer was obvious. She still didn't have her father figured out. He said he didn't want her involved in his case, yet he'd summoned her to the jail and swore he knew nothing about Talia Wind's murder. He had to be secretly hoping she'd get involved, or why bother? Of course, that could just be the cynical part of her mind talking.

The other part, the part that was woman and daughter, wanted to believe he'd asked for her because he'd missed their first scheduled meeting in twenty-five years, and he wanted to be sure she understood he couldn't help it.

Realistically, it hardly mattered why he'd wanted to see her. Nor did his insistence that he didn't want her involved. She couldn't help being involved. He was a suspect in the murder she was investigating.

"Molly?" D.J. queried, jerking her mind back to him.

"Sorry. I was thinking . . ."

"Did he talk to you about the night Talia Wind was murdered?"

"He said he didn't know her, never even saw her, didn't know she was dead till he heard about it the next day. Said he heard her chanting while he was still outside the library, so he left. That must've been when she was doing the medicine ceremony. He probably didn't tell me anything he hasn't already told you."

"Right," he said, looking disappointed. "We could sure use a witness, somebody who saw him approach the library that night and then leave without breaking in."

"Nobody's around there at night."

"Except the murderer—that night."

Molly sighed. "True."

"Maybe we could put out a call for help in the newspaper, but I doubt Claude will buy it. It'd look like we're getting nowhere with the case."

"Which we aren't," she said.

He took her arm and walked her toward the door separating the hallway from the main foyer. A sign attached to the door said: "Keep Door Shut At All Times. Don't Forget Your Gun!" Deputies who rarely had to use a gun tended to forget them. Did they lock them out of sight in a glove compartment, like Molly?

D.J. opened the door and ushered her into the foyer. "I'm sorry it's turned out this way, sugar."

"Tell me the truth, D.J. Do you think Talia caught him breaking into the library and he killed her to keep her quiet?"

"No."

"What about Claude? He's pretty hard up for a suspect. Plus, I'm really on his bad side right now."

"Personally, I think what evidence we have points to the Beavers, one of them or both. But I can't speak for the Sheriff."

"Did he talk to Agasuyed Beaver after Ina came in?"

D.J. nodded. "Beaver says he had no idea his wife sent those notes or attacked Talia. And he flatly denied being involved in the murder. He stuck to Ina's story that they were home together Sunday night."

Molly thought of something that might redeem her with the Sheriff. "Give the Sheriff a message for me. Tell him that Talia Wind was having an affair with Josh Rollins."

He looked stunned. "Whoa. Are you talking about the Rollins who owns the Silver Flame Steakhouse?"

"He's the guy."

"Are you sure?"

"Yes, and I think he's the man Talia was with the night she died. One of the women at Eagle Rock saw her leave the compound between eight and nine o'clock. My father says it was after midnight when he heard her chanting, which probably meant she hadn't been in the library long—she'd do the medicine ceremony first thing. I think she was with Josh Rollins before she went to the library. I wanted to talk to him today, but he was out of town. I'll go back tomorrow."

He frowned. "Can I tell Claude you'll check in with him first?"

She thought about it. It rankled but, with her father in custody, it seemed a good idea to be as cooperative as possible, in spite of the angry exchange she'd had with Hobart that day. It was time to eat some crow. "I'll phone him in the morning."

He walked with her to the courthouse door. "I need to find out who's up for public defender," she said.

"Your dad ask you to do that?"

"No, he said he wanted me to stay out of it." She opened the door. "I can't do that."

He stepped outside with her and pulled her to him for a kiss. She wound her arms around his neck and relaxed against him for a long moment, getting into the kiss, letting it dim the worries that filled her mind.

But when the kiss ended, the worries rushed back, like water filling the vacuum where a boulder had been.

"Try to get some sleep, sweetheart," he said.

That wasn't likely, but she said, "I will." Walking to her car, she glanced back, saw the lighted foyer behind the glass doors. D.J. had gone inside. She thought of her father in a cell and looked toward the jail. A dim light shone in a cell window. A man's head was silhouetted in the narrow frame. It was her father. She was glad they'd given him a window.

✳ ✳ ✳

The phone rang as she stepped into the apartment. Homer pushed in after her and she grabbed the receiver. "Hello."

"Home already?" It was Eva.

"Just walked in."

"Did Rob ever show up at the café?"

"No, but I talked to him." Molly went on to explain what had happened.

Eva was silent for a long moment before she said, "The emphysema must be pretty bad if he's getting disability."

"I gather it's worse some times than others."

"What's going to happen to him?"

"I'll know more after the hearing. I don't think the Sheriff can make a murder charge stick with what he has now."

"He could have stayed with me for a while," Eva muttered.

"He wouldn't have felt welcome. Besides, I think he was too proud to ask." Molly walked around the table, stretching the phone cord to its limit, and kicked the door closed. Homer flopped down in front of the door and watched her.

"He told me something that surprised me, Grandmother," Molly went on. "He said he wanted to keep in touch with me after Mama died, but you asked him not to."

Silence stretched between them until finally Eva cleared her throat and said, "I've always been afraid you'd find out about that."

"Why did you do it, Grandmother?"

"I told myself it was the best thing for you at the time, and I guess I wanted to believe I had only your good at heart."

"I'm sure you did, but—"

"No, that wasn't all of it. I was so mad at him, for leaving like he did, and I blamed him for Josie's death. I wanted to make him hurt like I was hurting."

"I think he was hurting plenty already."

"Later, when I'd had time to think it over, I was sorry I'd done it. But I didn't know how to get in touch with him. I should have told you about it long ago. I should've known you had to find out sometime."

"You never wanted to talk about anything that had to do with my parents."

"Maybe that was a mistake, too. I'm an old woman and I've made plenty of mistakes in my time. But telling Rob to stay out of your life was a big one, and you're the one who paid for it."

She'd paid big-time, in anger and resentment and feelings of abandonment.

Eva went on in a small voice, "Can you forgive me, Molly?"

What choice did she have? She couldn't hold any more grudges, deal with any more pain. It was all ancient history, anyway. "It was a long time ago, Grandmother. And who knows what I'd have done in your place."

She expelled a breath. "You're a good girl, Molly. Now, I'm gonna have to go see Rob at the jail, ask his forgiveness, too. I never visited anybody in jail before."

"I'd rather you didn't go. It's not an experience I'd wish on anybody."

"Have to. Can't be helped."

"He can only have visitors on Wednesday afternoons."

"I'll go tomorrow then."

"I'll come and get you."

"No. Opal Trynor does her grocery shopping on Wednesdays. I'll get a ride with her."

"If that's what you want, Grandmother."

You have put the Intruder into a crevice in a high mountain,
that it may never find the way back.

15

Molly woke up the next morning with a vague, nagging pain between her eyes that reminded her she'd spent more of the night staring into the dark than sleeping.

After Eva's call, she'd fed Homer and let him stay in for the night. Her temporarily absent landlord, Conrad Swope, had built Homer a snug doghouse, where he usually spent the night. But when Molly had gone to the door to let him out, he'd sprawled on his stomach with his head resting on his paws and rolled big, pleading eyes up at her. The thought of Homer's loving, nonjudgmental canine company had been comforting.

She'd made a ham sandwich with thick slices of homemade whole wheat bread, poured a tall glass of milk, and talked to Homer as she ate. She gave him the crust scraps when she finished, which he gulped down as though he had no idea where his next meal was coming from.

Then she'd sunk into a chair and picked up her weaving. She'd taken a course the previous winter in the ancient art of Cherokee finger weaving. The only equipment required was a dowel and a big safety pin. She found the activity restful. So far she'd made a couple of belts, neither of which she liked well enough to wear. Her current project was more ambitious, wider than the belts with more than a hundred lengths of yarn in four colors to be manipulated. She was trying to duplicate an ancient Peruvian design from a color photograph in one of her weaving books. The design created the illusion of interlocking diagonal bands. With no pattern and little experience, she'd done a lot of unraveling and reweaving. If the piece turned out well, she'd hang it on the wall over the couch.

As her hands worked the yarn, she watched a tragic drama on television having to do with a parent kidnapping a child, then caught the nightly news on a Tulsa station, which recounted more tragedies closer to home.

She'd done a fair job of blotting her father out of her mind, until she'd turned off the television, put aside the weaving, and gone to bed. In the periods of wakefulness during the night, she'd thought about Talia Wind's death and the people who might have been involved in it, including her father.

Agasuyed Beaver wanted to be rid of Talia because she was challenging his spiritual leadership of the Eagle Rock community.

Ina Beaver wanted Talia out because she was a continual thorn in Agasuyed's side, and constant agitation was a health threat to him.

Dell Greer had wanted Talia to leave Eagle Rock for the

same reasons that Ina did, and one or two of his own. He couldn't leave his trailer without seeing Talia's mobile home; it was like being hit in the face with Talia's obstinacy and the divorce, which he hadn't wanted.

Josh Rollins had been having an affair with Talia. Was it just a married man's little fling, or something more? What if Talia had started making demands, insisted that he talk to Belinda about a divorce or she, Talia, would. If Rollins was the man Talia was with Sunday night, maybe they argued and when she left him, he followed her to the library to continue the discussion. Maybe the argument got out of hand, and he strangled her. Maybe.

And then there was Rollins's wife, who may have had the strongest motive of all to get rid of Talia.

Which brought Molly to her father, who had had the bad luck to be in the wrong place at the wrong time, and only his word that he left the library that night without ever seeing Talia.

Molly went through the list of names over and over during the night, wondering what she'd missed. Whatever it was, she didn't find it.

Now it was time to do something—anything.

She got out of bed, let Homer out, ground some Kona beans and started coffee brewing. Then she rummaged in the cabinet for her rarely used waffle iron and fixed breakfast. Sitting at the small table, she looked out on a pale blue sky behind leafy tree branches. It was clear and going to be another perfect, warmish day edging closer to real summer, which always seemed to descend on northeast Oklahoma in one day on a sudden blast of heat.

It was after eight by the time she'd washed the few breakfast dishes and dressed in khaki jeans and a brown-and-green cotton shirt. She called the Sheriff's office from her apartment. Hobart, alerted by D.J., had been expecting her call and surprised her by grumbling, "Sorry about your father."

"What are you charging him with?"

"Breaking and entering."

"Is that all?"

"For now. He'll probably get off pretty easy if nothing else comes up. He didn't steal or damage anything. The hearing's tomorrow afternoon. It might not even go to trial. Depends on how hard-nosed the DA's going to be." Her information about Talia's lover seemed to have made him more cooperative. Or maybe it was her threat that she would go around him and conduct her own investigation. "About Josh Rollins," he went on, "you real sure he's the guy Talia was with?"

"I'm sure she was having an affair with him. She was with somebody that night. Seems logical it was him."

Hobart grunted, and Molly knew he didn't relish the idea of confronting a prominent citizen. "Better talk to him, then."

"When?"

"Sometime today."

She'd give him one more chance to let her in on his investigation. "I was planning to talk to him myself. I'd rather do it with you than on my own." Being in the Sheriff's company would give her credibility.

"Hell, since you're going to talk to him, anyway, I'd rather be there. How about two o'clock?"

"I'll come by the courthouse and ride with you, if that's okay."

He grunted an assent, then a curt goodbye, and hung up.

She'd no sooner replaced the receiver when the phone rang. It was Tim Dowell.

"Got the estimate on your car, Molly."

She groaned. "Should I sit down?"

He chuckled. "Maybe you ought to. It ain't good. We could do the whole thing for nine hundred fifty, but I have to say I'd hate to see you spend that much on a vehicle carrying so much mileage. When things start going wrong with these old cars, there's no end."

"I hear you," she said. "I guess I better think about it."

"We can fix you up with that Accord you're driving. Stretch the payments out so they won't hurt so much. I ran some figures before I called you. How does two hundred a month grab you?"

Molly could live with that. "Not bad."

"You mull it over and let me know."

"I could come by today—later this morning, maybe."

"Whenever. I'll be here till five, maybe later. Springtime brings out the shoppers."

Molly had left the morning free to pursue an idea she'd had in the middle of the night. By the light of day, it seemed less promising, but it was the only thing she could think to do at the moment. Maybe she should have mentioned it to Tim, but he might nix the idea to protect his father.

During the night, she'd thought some more about what Rayburn Dowell had said the day her Civic had conked out, something about seeing the ghost go through the wall at the Native American Research Library. Only, she didn't think he'd actually said "ghost," because she'd wondered if he meant a man. But she and Tim had been talking about the ghost and Rayburn had said "he" went through the wall.

Tim had brushed it off as an Alzheimer's delusion. But he'd also said he'd had to bring his father down to the dealership at night a few times. Now that she knew about that loose stone, it was possible that Rayburn really *had* seen something—maybe he'd seen her father entering the library.

Then it had occurred to her that Rayburn Dowell had been wandering around town the night Talia Wind was murdered. When found, he'd said he'd been looking for Tim, who was at home in bed. Evidently it hadn't occurred to Rayburn to look there, but he might have looked for his son at the dealership. And maybe he'd seen her father approach the library and leave without going in.

It was a long shot, but worth going out to the Dowell house in Rambling Oaks and talking to the old man.

After passing through the stone-pillared entry to the upscale addition, Molly drove along gently curving streets looking for the address she'd found in the phone book. In spite of the addition's name, she didn't see many oaks around. Come to think of it, how could oaks ramble, anyway?

The Dowell house was a low, limestone ranch with hunter green shutters. It sat on a half-acre corner lot. There was an old Mercury parked in the driveway, presumably belonging to the woman who cared for Rayburn Dowell while Tim was at work.

None of the houses in the addition were older than eight or ten years. Tim had said the house was his, that his father had given it to him. It must have been built when Tim's mother was alive, when his father was still running the dealership. Rayburn had probably deeded the house to Tim when he was told that he had Alzheimer's. It would keep Tim from having to go through probate to get it when his father died.

As Molly pulled over to park at the curb, she caught sight of Rayburn Dowell sitting on a bench in the backyard, which was fenced with chain link. She walked around the house and opened the gate, securing it behind her. He was just sitting there, with a folded newspaper beside him. He saw her coming and a half-wary, half-puzzled expression came over his face.

"Good morning, Mr. Dowell," Molly said cheerily.

There was no recognition in his eyes. His expression didn't change.

"I'm Molly Bearpaw. We met the other day at the car dealership. You were with Tim. Remember?"

He nodded, still looking vague. She didn't think he remembered her.

The back door of the house opened and a large, middle-aged woman leaned out. "Hello. Can I help you?"

Molly walked over to the door. "I'm Molly Bearpaw, a friend of Tim's." She extended her hand.

"I'm Helen Carmichael. I look after Mr. Dowell for Tim."

"Tim told me what a big help you are to him." Helen Carmichael flushed at the compliment. "I was driving by and saw Mr. Dowell sitting out here," Molly went on. "Thought I'd stop and say hello."

"Oh, good. He gets hardly any company anymore." She shook her head sadly. "Most of the time, he doesn't remember people, even friends he's known for years. So they stopped coming. Tim and I carry on conversations with him all the time, even when he doesn't respond. Maybe it helps, I don't know."

"Tim loves his father very much."

"He's a good son. Too good, I sometimes think. Hardly ever goes out in the evening. I've been telling him there's more to life than work and duty. Finally convinced him. He asked me if I could sleep in the guest room last night because he wanted to go out to dinner and a late movie. Of course I was glad to do it. A young man like Tim needs a social life." She glanced at Rayburn Dowell, who was still sitting on the bench, watching the two of them. She lowered her voice. "I'm sure Tim was with a young woman last night, though he didn't tell me her name. Of course, I would never pry." She eyed Molly thoughtfully. "Wouldn't happen to have been you, would it?"

Molly laughed. "No, and I have no idea who it was. I didn't know Tim was seeing someone, but I'm glad if he is."

She looked disappointed. Contrary to her claim that she would never pry, Molly thought she probably kept pretty close tabs on her employer as well as her charge. It was killing her that she didn't know who Tim was with the night before. Whoever the woman was, her appearance in Tim's life must be very recent. Only days ago, Tim had asked Molly out. But Tim Dowell would have no trouble finding female companionship. Molly hoped he'd found somebody who would appreciate him.

"Listen, honey," Helen Carmichael said, "if you plan to stay awhile, I could run out to the store. We're out of milk and I want to make a coconut cream pie. It'd only take fifteen minutes."

"Sure. I can stay that long."

"Oh, good. I can't leave him alone, you know. Even when he's in the backyard, I have to keep an eye on him. Lately he's been wandering off." She hesitated. "You sure you don't mind?"

"Not at all. You go on. I'll sit in the yard with Mr. Dowell."

"Thank you. I'll just run and get my purse."

Rayburn Dowell watched her as she walked over to the bench and sat down beside him. "It's a nice day to be outside," Molly said.

He didn't answer, but he nodded, which was encouraging. His eyes continued to search her face.

"Tim's letting me drive one of the dealership's cars. I think I'm going to buy it."

Intelligence flickered in his eyes, where before there had been a blank look. It must've been the mention of his son that did it. "Tim is a good boy," he said.

"Yes, he is. And Mrs. Carmichael seems very nice, too."

"Helen."

"That's right. Helen Carmichael."

"Helen," he said again.

Enough chitchat, Molly thought. He could disappear into his head at any time. She wanted to question him while he was still with her.

"You remember you told me you saw somebody go through the wall at the Native American Research Library—the old jail?"

"He went through the wall," Dowell said.

"That's right. I think you saw a homeless man who's been sleeping in the library. They caught him."

He smiled faintly, as though at some private joke.

"Mr. Dowell, do you remember the night you got lost and

ended up in the town park? You went to sleep on a picnic table."

"I couldn't find Tim," he said.

"Do you remember where you went before you went to the park? Did you go to the dealership—to your office—looking for Tim?"

He frowned. "They leave the lights on in the garage."

"At the car dealership?"

"The mechanics don't care. They don't pay the electric bill." He leaned toward her.

"Did you see the lights on in the garage the night you were looking for Tim?"

"They leave the lights on. I told on them. I told Tim."

Had he really gone to the dealership that night, or was he remembering another time? He sounded fairly lucid, but Molly had talked to total psychotics who sounded perfectly sane—for a while.

"Did you see anyone that night?"

He gripped the edge of the bench with both hands. He was getting agitated. The veins in his neck stood out and his face was red. "They leave the lights on."

"Yes, I know. But did you see anybody around the library?"

He gripped the bench harder. "They don't care." Suddenly, he stood, making Molly jump. For an instant, she thought he might strike out at her. But he turned his back and walked toward the house. She'd lost him.

Molly caught up with him, followed him inside. He looked around as though he didn't recognize the combination den-kitchen. "Helen's gone to the store," she said. "I'll stay with you till she gets back."

One end of the big room was furnished with heavy, South-western pieces arranged around a massive stone fireplace. A breakfast bar separated the den from the kitchen, with its oak cabinets and wallpaper depicting rustic outdoor scenes and hunting dogs. All very masculine. She wondered if this was how Mrs. Dowell had left it, or had Tim and his father redecorated after her death?

Molly noticed the red light on the coffeemaker. The glass pot was half-full. "Would you like a cup of coffee?"

He nodded, but continued to look around as though searching for something familiar. Molly took hold of his arm. "You sit down and I'll get your coffee."

He allowed her to lead him to a chair. She found a mug in the cabinet and poured it half-full of coffee. She placed the mug in his hands. He accepted it and watched her carefully as she sat down on the couch.

She smiled. "You have a lovely home."

He cocked his head, as if listening to some faraway sound. Then, slowly, he slumped down in the chair and rested his head on the back. She jumped up and grabbed the mug before he dropped it. She took it to the kitchen. When she came back, Rayburn Dowell's eyes were closed and he seemed to be sleeping.

He didn't stir again and about twenty minutes later Helen Carmichael returned. She came into the kitchen, carrying a grocery sack, which she set on the counter, her eyes anxiously searching out her charge.

"Any problems?" she asked.

"No. He fell asleep right after you left," Molly said.

She made a clucking sound. "The old dear. He does that sometimes, just lays his head back and he's gone." She pulled a half-gallon container of milk from the grocery sack and put it in the refrigerator. "Lately, he's gotten physical with me a few times. Nothing serious, but I told Tim I won't be able to handle him if he turns really violent. Tim's going to ask the doctor for sedatives to calm him when he gets like that."

Now she tells me, Molly thought, remembering that moment in the yard when she'd thought Rayburn Dowell meant to hit her. Of course, if Helen Carmichael had told her before her trip to the store, Molly wouldn't have wanted to stay with the man alone. Which may have been why Helen hadn't told her about his behavior.

"I'd better be going," Molly said.

Helen Carmichael saw her to the door. "Thank you for helping me out, dear."

"No problem," Molly told her.

As she drove away from the Dowell house, she thought about what the Carmichael woman had told her. Rayburn Dowell was getting to be a problem for her, getting physical, violent.

Molly's imagination constructed a scenario in which the elder Dowell walked to the dealership Sunday night, bewildered, confused, frightened—angry—looking for his son, whom he'd left at home in bed. He noticed that the mechanics had left the lights on in the garage again, which fueled his anger. Talia Wind heard him stumbling around, talking to himself, shouting perhaps. She came out of the library and confronted him and, suddenly, she became the focus of all of Rayburn Dowell's rage and confusion. Maybe he thought she was hiding Tim. Maybe he thought she was one of the mechanics. Whatever he thought, he strangled her, left her dead or dying, and wandered back to town with no memory of what he'd done.

As a scenario, it was all smoke and mirrors, Molly mused as she drove. No way to prove any of it. An even bigger problem was the fact that the murderer had put Talia on the gallows after he killed her in an effort to make it look like suicide. Did Rayburn Dowell have enough logical thought process left to even think of covering up the murder?

You have put it to rest in the Darkening Land,
so that it may never return.
Let the relief come.

16

A half-hour later, Molly sat in Tim Dowell's office signing papers that made the Accord hers—and the bank's until she paid off the note.

"That's the last one," Tim said, reaching for the paper she'd just signed. "You got yourself a good little car." He was chewing on a toothpick.

"Thanks for letting me drive it till I made up my mind."

"Glad to." He tossed the papers into a box on his desk and leaned back in his chair. "So, what's new with you?"

"I finally saw my father. He's in jail."

"Aw, Molly, I'm sorry. What happened?"

She told him the whole story, winding up with, "There's a hearing tomorrow. He'll be charged with breaking and entering, but I don't think they can tie him to Talia Wind's murder."

He frowned. "God, I hope not. I'll keep a good thought for ya." He shook his head. "Parents. Right?"

"Speaking of parents, I went out to see your dad this morning."

He worried the toothpick around in his mouth. "Oh?"

"I had a crazy idea," she explained. "Remember your dad said he saw somebody go through the wall at the library?"

He tossed the toothpick into the wastebasket beside his desk. "If I took seriously everything my dad says these days, I'd drive myself crazy. He's delusional half the time."

"I know, but after I found out my father has been sleeping in the library, I thought maybe your father really did see him breaking in. And then I thought maybe he saw him approach the library and leave again immediately the night Talia Wind was murdered. That was the night he was wandering around town."

He pulled out a desk drawer and extracted another toothpick. "They found him in Town Branch Park, nowhere near the library."

"Yeah, I know. It was a desperation move on my part."

He smiled sympathetically and held up the toothpick. "What I really want is a candy bar, but I'm trying to shuck ten pounds." He popped the toothpick into his mouth. "Did Dad recognize you?"

"No."

"Let me guess. You didn't get a word out of him. He clams up like that all the time."

"Oh, he talked, but it didn't make much sense. Kept saying they leave the lights on in the garage."

"They?"

"I think he meant your mechanics, but I'm not sure. He said he told you about it. It seemed to really agitate him, so I didn't want to keep talking about it."

He looked puzzled, then laughed. "Can't remember him

getting on that lately, but he always did think the mechanics wasted supplies, left the lights on, stuff like that. Even before he got sick. He must've warned me a hundred times to keep an eye on them when I took over the dealership."

"I got the impression he was talking about the night he ran away."

He shrugged. "Like I said, you never know. He gets confused about days and dates. Of course, the garage lights could've been on that night. Wouldn't be the first time. I don't always remember to check after the mechanics leave for the day. But, like I said, I don't think he walked all the way out here and then back to town again."

She nodded. He was probably right, though it wasn't an impossibility. Dowell could've had all night to walk to the dealership and back to town—there was no way of knowing when he left his house. But it *was* a long walk, and nothing Rayburn Dowell said could be taken as fact. She reached for her purse and stood.

Tim got up and walked outside with her. "Listen, you have any problems with that Accord, bring it back. We'll make it right."

"Thanks, I will."

He followed her outside and waved to her from the door of the dealership.

She had lunch before going to the office, where she found Natalie, seated at her desk, and Ridge perched on the desktop.

He smiled at Molly as she entered. "Hi."

"Hi, yourself."

Ridge cleared his throat. "We're real sorry about your dad, Molly."

"Thanks."

"He didn't bother anything in the library," Ridge went on.

Molly nodded. "It was a stupid idea, hiding out there, not telling anyone that he needed a place to stay." She glanced at Natalie, who appeared even more tired than she had yesterday. Molly tossed her purse on her desk and pointed a finger at her assistant. "You go home."

"That's what I've been trying to tell her," Ridge said. "Maybe she'll listen to you. I have to get back to work now." He slid off the desk. "She's losing it, Molly." He opened the door, looked back at his sister. "Tell her what you did last night."

Molly gazed at the closed door for a moment, before returning her attention to Natalie. "Well?"

Natalie yawned hugely. "What?"

"What about last night?"

"Let me put it this way. A car's not a very comfortable place to spend the night." Natalie's was a subcompact.

"And where was your car?"

Natalie grimaced. "On that side road, near the Native American Library. I parked where I could watch the library."

Molly stared at her. "What on earth—oh, wait, let me guess. You wanted to catch the murderer returning to the scene of the crime."

Natalie had the grace to blush. "I couldn't sleep, anyway, so I might as well have been there as tossing in my bed."

Molly went around her desk and plopped into her chair. "What happened?"

Natalie shrugged. "Not a thing. The place was like a tomb all night, and once I got there, I kept dozing off. I can't really say if anything happened while I was sleeping. I stayed till dawn. Came within an inch of being sideswiped by a Mercedes when I started back to town. I guess I was punch-drunk by then. Didn't even see it until it passed me. It was like it came out of nowhere. Sure woke me up, I can tell you that." She yawned again and pushed her chair away from her desk. "You know, I think I will go back to the dorm and lie down. I'm not much good to anybody this way. I probably won't be back till next week. Ridge and I are driving to Idabel tomorrow afternoon for Aunt Talia's funeral on Friday."

"No problem, Nat. And concentrate on your finals when you get back. I can cope around here till the semester's over."

She pushed herself out of her chair and went to the door.

"Nat," Molly said as she opened it. "That Mercedes you saw. It didn't happen to be baby blue, did it?"

Natalie gave her an odd look. "Nope. It was dark red, sort of wine. Why?"

Molly shook her head. "Just a crazy thought I had. You take care now."

Natalie nodded tiredly and left.

Shortly after two that afternoon, Josh Rollins ushered Molly and the Sheriff into his office at the Silver Flame. His wife, Belinda, who was working at a desk in the outer office, tracked them suspiciously with her eyes until Rollins closed his office door.

Molly and Hobart took the two blue-upholstered chairs that Rollins offered. Instead of going behind his desk, he perched on the edge of the high-backed deacon's bench facing his visitors. Appropriate, Molly thought wryly. A deacon's bench for Deacon Rollins.

Rollins was probably in his late forties, tall and lean. His face with its prominent bones and long jaw missed handsomeness by a mere fraction. His Indian blood was evident in his crooked nose and nearly black eyes.

Resting his forearms on his thighs, he dangled his hands between his knees. He had readily agreed to talk to them, but now he seemed nervous.

"So," he said, with forced heartiness, "what can I do for the law this afternoon?"

Molly, who had decided to let Hobart take the lead, waited for him to reply.

The Sheriff scooted forward in his chair and spoke in a confidential tone. "It's come to our attention, Mr. Rollins, that you were—um, acquainted with the late Talia Wind."

Rollins placed his hands on his knees, elbows thrusting outward. "My wife and I knew Ms. Wind, yes. We attended the same church."

Molly glanced at Hobart, who shifted in his chair. "According to our information, you knew her better than your wife did, Mr. Rollins."

He studied his cordovan loafers for a moment before meeting the Sheriff's gaze. "I'm not sure I understand what you're getting at, Sheriff." He could lie with a straight face.

Hobart shifted again and cast an uncertain look in Molly's direction. She wasn't about to let Rollins off that easily. She stepped in and with more bluntness than the Sheriff seemed prepared to use. "We have evidence that you were with Talia Wind the night she was murdered." A gross exaggeration, but Rollins had no way of knowing that. They had evidence that

Talia had been with a man shortly before her death, but they couldn't prove it was Rollins without a DNA test.

He darted a worried look at the closed door, painfully aware that his wife sat on the other side and surely had an ear cocked toward the office. Rollins stood, walked to the office window, and gazed out. Then he turned back to Molly and Hobart. "My wife knows nothing about that, and I'd like to keep it that way." He spoke so low that Molly had to strain to hear. She felt a little sorry for him. If Belinda Rollins didn't know about her husband's affair with Talia, she would before the investigation was over. But, remembering the look Belinda had given Talia at the wild onion breakfast, Molly suspected she already knew.

"You admit you were with her that night?" Hobart asked.

Rollins sat back down. He seemed to debate his answer with himself before he finally said, "Yes," with another look at the door, "and please keep your voice down." He looked different, depleted somehow, from when Molly had first seen him, as if some vital energy had gone out of him since Sunday.

"Tell us about Sunday night," Molly said.

He took a deep breath. "We met here," he said in the same low voice, "about nine. We close at eight on Sundays. Belinda thinks I was working late. It was close to midnight when Talia left, and I went home."

"And you never saw Talia or talked to her again after that?" Hobart asked.

He shook his head. "I found out the next afternoon, after I came to the restaurant, that she was dead."

"What happened after you and Talia separated and you went home?" Molly asked.

He frowned at the question. "Nothing. I went to bed."

"With your wife?"

His frown deepened. "No—I didn't want to wake her. The master bedroom is upstairs. We have a guest room downstairs, and I slept there. I often do that when I come home late."

After being with Talia Wind, Molly thought, remembering the comfortable-looking, extra-long sofa in the outer office. "So you didn't see your wife at all until the next morning?"

He seemed disturbed by Molly's persistence. "That's right."

"How long had this thing with Talia Wind been going on?" Hobart asked.

"A few months. We met—at church. She was having a debate with Reverend McCall when I first saw her." He gazed toward the window with a faraway look. "She was the most interesting woman I ever knew. The first few times we met, we just talked—for hours." He looked at the Sheriff. "I thought that would be enough. I never set out to have an affair."

Hobart looked uncomfortable and mumbled something unintelligible. Molly waited, watching Rollins.

There was a long silence. Rollins slumped against the back of the wood bench. "I married the wrong woman," he announced in a dull, resigned voice. After a moment, he seemed to shake himself, and he straightened up, leaned forward, and briefly covered his face with his hands. "I was young, too inexperienced to know that constant mothering attention and meaningless chatter would wear thin very quickly. I've considered divorce many times, but it would devastate Belinda. And untangling one or both of us from the business would be a nightmare." He lifted his head and looked at the Sheriff. "I decided to stick it out. It wasn't so hard before I met Talia."

Hobart lifted an eyebrow.

"No man should get married before he's thirty," Rollins observed softly.

Hobart cleared his throat. "Well . . ." Molly had heard that the Sheriff had married right out of high school.

Before Hobart could disagree with Rollins and derail his train of thought, Molly said, "You and Talia talked of marriage?"

He shook his head. "Not exactly. Not directly. But she knew how I felt about her. Talia was the only woman I ever really loved. I—I don't know what would have happened eventually—we'd have worked something out, I suppose."

Which could mean a lot of things.

So, Molly thought, Talia was his one true love. Touching. But had he really been prepared to divorce his wife and marry Talia—risk losing the business, not to mention his status as an upstanding, churchgoing pillar of the community?

"Did Talia ever talk about being afraid of somebody—anybody in particular?"

He smiled sadly. "Her ex-husband and Agasuyed Beaver were giving her a hard time, but I wouldn't say Talia was afraid of them. She was very strong, handled her own problems—without making a big deal out of it, if you know what I mean. Not the type to whine or cling." He glanced toward the door as if he'd reminded himself that the woman on the other side *was* the type. "Lord, was that refreshing! It was one of the many things I admired about Talia. She—"

Suddenly, his voice broke. He pressed his lips together and fought back tears.

When Rollins had composed himself, Molly and Hobart continued to question him. Had Talia mentioned anybody at Eagle Rock when they were together Sunday night? Had she

told him about the anonymous notes she'd received? Had he
noticed anybody around the restaurant or a car parked nearby,
when Talia left him to go to the library? He answered nega-
tively to all the questions.

"We'd like to talk to your wife," Molly said as they prepared to leave the office.

Rollins halted with his hand on the knob of the closed
door. "Is that really necessary?"

"Yes," Molly said. "She knew Talia, too."

He looked at Molly and then the Sheriff. "You'll be careful what you say to her?"

Hobart nodded and gave Rollins a comforting pat on the
shoulder, man to man.

Molly raised an eyebrow at the Sheriff and said nothing.

They filed out of the office behind Josh Rollins. Belinda
looked up from her work. "The Sheriff and Ms. Bearpaw
would like to talk to you, Belinda," Rollins said.

Her pale, lightly freckled face seemed to Molly to go another shade paler, but the light in the office wasn't bright, so
she could've been mistaken.

Belinda Rollins was too thin for her height and wore her
brown hair cut very short, which made her long neck look
even longer. She put down the pen she'd been holding. "What
about?"

Hobart looked at Molly. "We're investigating the murder
of Talia Wind, Mrs. Rollins. We're talking to as many of the
people who knew her as we can."

She glanced quickly at her husband, who walked over and
stood behind her chair. He placed a hand on her shoulder. "I
told them we knew her from church, dear—but not well."

Molly frowned. She didn't appreciate Rollins coaching his wife.

"That's right," Belinda said. "I only talked to her once or twice."

"What was your impression of her?" Molly asked.

An odd stillness settled on Belinda's face, making it almost masklike. "I thought she had a screw loose," she said.

A muscle in Rollins's jaw twitched, but his wife couldn't see that since he was standing behind her.

"What made you think that?" Molly asked.

"Huh." Belinda snorted. "She was into some weird Indian magic stuff. Talked about it in front of the preacher and anybody else who would listen. I heard that people actually paid her to do readings from a deck of Indian medicine cards. Like a fortune-teller, I guess. She was nuts, but smart enough to get paid for feeding gullible people a lot of nonsense."

Molly saw Rollins's hand tighten on his wife's shoulder. She winced and looked up at him. "I'm merely answering their questions as truthfully as I can, Josh."

"The woman's dead," Rollins muttered between his teeth.

Belinda shrugged carelessly. "That doesn't change my opinion of her."

"Mrs. Rollins," Hobart said, "I understand your husband worked late Sunday night." She dipped her head slightly. Hobart went on, "Were you awake when he got home?"

She no longer looked careless, she'd become alert. "Sunday night-..." she said slowly. "Isn't that the night Talia—" She broke off.

"The night Talia was killed," Molly finished for her. "According to your husband, he was at the office until close to midnight. Did you know when he came home?"

"No. I went to bed about ten, and I'm a very sound sleeper. But I don't understand what that has to do with your investigation."

She was dimmer than Molly thought she was if she didn't know exactly what it had to do with it. "It'll help us locate possible witnesses if we know where all of Talia's acquaintances were when she was murdered."

"Witnesses!"

"It's all right, Belinda," Rollins said, though he didn't sound very confident.

"Were you at home all evening last Sunday, Mrs. Rollins?"

"Yes, of course. Where else would I be?"

Checking on your husband's whereabouts, Molly thought. Stalking Talia, tailing her to the Native American Research Library? Molly had no trouble at all imagining Belinda following Talia and confronting her at the library. Rollins had admitted that he didn't go into their bedroom when he got home Sunday night, that he didn't see his wife until the next morning at breakfast. If Belinda was following Talia, she'd have been out of the house when Josh got home. Could she have slipped back in without her husband hearing her?

Hobart cleared his throat and said suddenly, "We'll be going now. Thank you for your cooperation, Mrs. Rollins. And you, Mr. Rollins."

Molly would have pressed a little harder, but she kept her mouth shut. Josh Rollins looked vastly relieved that they were leaving.

Returning to the courthouse in the Sheriff's car, Molly said, "Belinda Rollins knew about the affair."

Hobart looked over at her sharply. "How do you know?"

"You saw her reaction to the mere mention of Talia's name. She hated her. You don't hate somebody you hardly know because you think she's kooky."

"In other words, you *think* she knew about the affair. You don't know it."

"Belinda could have been checking up on her husband Sunday night. If she went to the restaurant looking for him, she saw Talia's car. She could have followed Talia to the library."

"So could a lot of other people," Hobart retorted. "Her ex-husband, for one."

"I don't know," Molly mused. "Talia was an irritant to Dell Greer, but I didn't get the feeling he despised her. He sure didn't give off hate vibes like Belinda."

"Vibes," Hobart said. "That'd go over big in court. Especially since you got a vested interest in proving the killer was somebody not related to you."

Molly let that go and said, "Speaking of that, my father will need a public defender. Do you know who's likely to be assigned?"

"No, and Judge Dreilling probably won't even think about that until the hearing tomorrow."

"I had hoped to be able to talk to the attorney before the case comes to court."

He glanced sideways at her. "Who knows? Your old man might get lucky. I've known Dreilling to hold the hearing and try the case immediately afterward. Depends on whether the public defender assigned to the case has had time to talk to the defendant. I talked to your father's friend, by the way, the one he was playing cards with Sunday night. The friend confirms that he left his house about midnight. So that part of his story checks out."

"That's good news."

"As an alibi, it's not much good. He admits he went to the library from his friend's house. We have only his word for what happened after that."

Molly stared straight ahead.

"One mystery's been solved, though," Hobart continued. "All that cockamamie stuff about hearing a ghost in the library. They heard your dad. Everything else was somebody's overworked imagination."

That had occurred to Molly, too. Some of the noises library employees heard, when working late, could have been made by her father. Sliding that big stone across the concrete floor could have sounded like the scraping of chairs, for example. But her father hadn't touched the computer—there was no reason for him to have lied about that. Nor could the reflection Alice Mundy saw in the glass door be explained so easily. Could those things be put down to somebody's overworked imagination?

Listen! Ha! Now you have drawn near to hearken;
You repose on high, O White Raven.
You never fail in anything.

17

The hearing the next day took place on the third floor of the courthouse building in the courtroom of District Judge Dreilling. Rob Bearpaw was represented by a young attorney named Dorfmeyer. Though Molly had not been able to find out who would represent her father before the hearing, Dorfmeyer seemed competent and had evidently talked with his client at length before the hearing, which lasted only a few minutes. When asked, Molly's father waived his right to a jury trial. After which, the judge asked both attorneys if they were prepared to try the case immediately. They were.

After hearing the evidence, Judge Dreilling reduced the breaking and entering charge to a misdemeanor and gave Rob Bearpaw six months probation. All very quick and easy.

The defendant was released immediately.

Molly talked to her father briefly. He hadn't expected to have his case resolved so quickly and seemed a little bewildered. He said he hoped never to go within a mile of a jail again. Molly hoped he never had to, but she knew that Hobart still considered him a suspect in Talia Wind's murder.

Her father said he was going straight to the bank to deposit his first disability check, and then he was going to find a place to rent.

"Would you like me to drive you?" Molly asked.

"No, I still have the pickup. You've probably got work to do, and I've been enough trouble to you already. Sorry about everything, Molly."

From his tone, she knew that everything included a lot more than his brush with the law. "It's okay."

"I'd still like to have that dinner," he said.

"Just say when."

"I'll call you as soon as I get settled."

They stood there, neither knowing what else to say or how they should part. Finally, Molly said, "Well, let me know where you'll be. Oh—" She fumbled in her purse for a business card. She wrote her home phone number on the back and handed it to him.

He looked at the card, then tucked it into his shirt pocket. He hesitated another moment, then said goodbye and left.

Oddly, she felt let down. She didn't know exactly why. But then her feelings about her father weren't exactly rational.

Having nothing more productive to do, Molly drove out to the Native American Library and found the side road leading off the main road, away from the library. She made a tight U-turn and parked on the shoulder where the road formed a T with the more heavily traveled road which bordered the library on one side and led to the highway.

This must be where her father had left his pickup at night while he slept in the library. It was also where Natalie must have parked last night. A car parked there probably would not be noticed by anybody traveling the intersecting road, and if it was, the driver would assume the owner had had car trouble and left the vehicle there temporarily.

From that location, Molly could see the library through the windshield to her right, although tall shrubs obscured the front of the building. The rear of the library was closer to her and she could see three cars parked near the back entrance, cars belonging to the three library employees. Visitors would park in front. Straight ahead was open ground with Dowell's Foreign Car showroom to her left but beyond her field of vision.

Molly sat in her car for several minutes, gazing at the library and wondering what she had hoped to learn by coming there.

Finally, she got out of her car and walked across the road. As she reached the opposite side, the car dealership came into view. She could see all of the showroom, which faced the road. The repair garages were partially hidden by the showroom, though she could see parts of two garages and an access road leading to them, making it possible to reach the garages without taking the main entrance and circling around the showroom.

She walked along the access road toward the garages. The door on the nearest one was open and several vehicles were parked outside. Two of the cars had been wrecked and needed extensive bodywork. A sign on the garage next to the repair and body shop identified it as the paint shop. Its door was closed.

She kept walking until her way was blocked by a gate wide enough to accommodate an eighteen-wheeler. The gate was secured by a heavy chain and padlock.

Molly turned back and walked around to the front of the library. She found Ridge Wind typing on the computer at the reception desk.

"I thought you and Natalie were going home this afternoon," Molly said.

"We're leaving at five, when I get off work." He turned away from the computer to face her. "Alice said the judge let your dad go with six months' probation. I know you're relieved."

The public defender had produced a statement by Alice Mundy, whom Molly could see shelving books in the reference room. The statement had said that nothing had been stolen from the library and no damage had been done.

Molly walked to the reference room door. "Alice." The librarian turned around and smiled when she saw Molly. "I wanted to thank you for your statement. I'm sure it was what tipped the scales in my father's favor."

"I only told the truth," Alice said. She frowned then. "Will he be staying with you?"

"He wants his own place," Molly told her. "He got a disability check, so he's looking for a rental today."

"Oh, good."

"Sorry for the scare he gave you."

"I think I scared him as much as he scared me. For a second there, I thought it was Ulenahiha." She shook her head. "But then I realized he was too—well, too solid to be a ghost." She glanced beyond Molly to where Ridge was working at the computer and lowered her voice. "We haven't heard any strange noises since Talia was here. Frankly, after I got over the shock of seeing your father in the basement, it was kind of a relief because now I think it was your father we heard coming or going on those nights we worked late. Of course, we haven't worked overtime lately, and I won't feel real sure until we put in a few evenings without hearing anything."

"Well, if it wasn't my father you heard," Molly said, smiling, "it's possible Talia's medicine ceremony worked."

"But at what a cost. I'm sorry we ever got her involved."

"You couldn't have foreseen what would happen."

Alice nodded. "You know, Deana is still convinced the ghost killed Talia." She glanced toward the stairs; evidently Deana was working in the basement. "But I don't believe that for a minute."

Nor did Molly.

Molly wondered, as she drove back to the office, what might have happened if Talia hadn't gone to the library to release the ghost. Would the murderer have found another time and place to kill her?

"Maybe," she murmured to herself as she pulled into her regular parking space at Cherokee Square. Or maybe the murder was an impulse, the result of an argument that got out of hand. Whoever did it had to have followed Talia to the library—or seen her car there and waited for her to come out. If the latter, it was somebody driving around after midnight, who was either looking for Talia or who merely happened upon her car by chance. Both Josh Rollins and Dell Greer had admitted to being out that night. Belinda Rollins and the Beavers claimed to have been home in bed at the time of the murder, but there was nothing but their word to prove that they were.

Apparently the killer had lured Talia outside—there was no evidence that she'd been killed in the library and, besides, Talia's flashlight was found near the gallows. For some reason, after Talia had performed the medicine ceremony, she'd left the library, taking the flashlight with her but leaving her carry-all and medicine paraphernalia in the basement. Obviously, she'd meant to return to the library.

Why had she gone outside?

Molly continued to mull over the question as she let herself into her office. She checked the answering machine. No messages. Two callers had hung up without speaking.

She got out the file folder she'd started for the Talia Wind investigation, leafed through the few notes she'd made, then closed the folder.

Gazing out the window, she asked herself again, Why had Talia gone outside that night?

Several possibilities came to mind. The killer had called her out. Had he first gone inside the library to talk to Talia? How had he gotten in? Either Talia had admitted him, or she'd left the door unlocked and he'd gone in unannounced. Would Talia have left the door unlocked? Molly didn't think so. She'd been receiving frightening anonymous threats and had even been physically attacked. She'd have been sure to lock the library door behind her.

Okay, then the killer had knocked on the door, she'd heard him from the basement, and had come upstairs to admit him. Or maybe he'd gone around and tapped on a basement window and she'd recognized him and gone up to let him in.

If Talia admitted her killer, then it was somebody she knew and trusted. Molly grabbed a memo pad and jotted down names. Who did Talia trust? Not the Beavers and probably not Dell Greer—she crossed those names out. Certainly not Molly's father. Talia didn't even know Rob Bearpaw. Molly crossed that name out, too. Would Talia have trusted Belinda Rollins? Maybe, if she believed that Belinda didn't know about the affair. Molly put a question mark beside Belinda's name.

The last name was Josh Rollins. Talia definitely would have trusted him—and any number of other people whose names weren't on the list because they had never been suspected of being implicated in the murder. The women in Talia's meditation groups, for example. Molly had discarded them as suspects long ago and now she did so again. No motive for any of them to want Talia dead had been found.

Frustrated, she threw down her pen.

She stared at Rollins's name. He and Talia would have worked something out, some way to be together, he'd said. He could have come up with a plan, after Talia left him at the restaurant, and had come to the library to discuss it with her. She would probably have followed him out as he was leaving, bringing the flashlight to light the way to his car.

And then what happened? Did they argue? Or did they part on good terms, Rollins driving away, leaving Talia alive and unharmed?

That would mean that somebody else was there after Rollins left. If Talia had had time to go back into the library, she would have locked the door behind her. But maybe Talia hadn't had time to get back inside. Maybe the killer had been watching, waiting for Rollins to leave before he approached Talia.

Molly groaned and put her head down on the desk. She had run out of maybes.

Ha! Now you are brought down.
There shall be left but a trace upon the ground where you have been.
Ha! Now you have taken it up.

18

Molly let herself and Homer in and opened a window to air out the apartment. D.J. had called just before she left the office for the last time that day, and they'd made a date for dinner. He wanted to try a new Mexican restaurant in Claremore, which was an hour's drive from Tahlequah, and would pick her up at six.

She fed Homer, then showered, dressed in jade leggings and a matching silk T-shirt, and pulled her hair back in a single French braid. By five-thirty, she was ready to go. She sat down at her computer, opened the Talia Wind file folder she'd brought home with her, and added the notes she'd made that day to the duplicate file in her computer. All of her active files were duplicated in her home computer. She liked to have them handy for perusing on the nights she couldn't get an investigation off her mind.

After typing in the day's notes, she scrolled through the file from the beginning, inserting additional details that she remembered as she went along. Then she read the whole file over from the beginning. There might be a clue buried there somewhere.

Thirty minutes later D.J. arrived.

"Wow, you look terrific." He gave her a long, slow kiss while Homer pushed his nose between their legs and whined for attention.

"You don't look so bad yourself, Deputy," she murmured breathlessly. It was moments like this when it really hit her how much she loved D.J. She still had to keep reminding herself that he was nothing like the man who'd destroyed her life, but it was getting easier.

D.J. bent down to scratch behind Homer's ears. "Hey, boy, how you doin'? I brought you something." He was wearing his uniform, as he had to go to work at midnight and might not have time to go back home and change. He reached into his shirt pocket and pulled out a cellophane-wrapped caramel. He unwrapped it and gave it to Homer, who chomped it right down and looked up for more.

"That's it, sport," Molly said, opening the door. "Out you go. Good dog."

Molly's chile rellenos dinner was outstanding and D.J. said the beef burritos were delicious, too.

"Glad we found this place," D.J. said. They had eaten and were lingering over coffee. "We'll have to come here again."

"Soon," Molly agreed.

"Have you heard from your dad since the hearing?"

Molly shook her head. "I think he wants to get moved into his own place before he makes contact." She sipped her coffee, set her cup down. "It's really weird, having him around."

"You'll be glad, once you get used to it."

She smiled. "I guess. We have to get acquainted before I can decide if I even like him or not."

"He seems like a nice guy to me."

"What are you, his press agent?"

He laughed and gestured to their waitress for more coffee. "I can put myself in his shoes easier than you can."

Molly reached for his hand across the table and laced her fingers through his. "When have you talked to Courtney?"

"A couple of days ago. She'll be out of school in less than a month. I made arrangements with Gloria to have her for a week in July when I take my vacation." He stared into his coffee cup. "Damn, I wish I could have her all summer."

"Would Gloria agree to that?"

"I've never asked. It's a moot point. There's nobody to leave Courtney with while I'm at work."

"You could find someone. Single parents do it all the time."

He gazed at their clasped hands and then at her. "You wouldn't mind?"

"Why should I mind?"

With his free hand, he covered their entwined fingers. "Do you really think it would work?"

"It's worth the effort to at least try to make it work. Courtney needs to spend more time with her father, D.J."

"And," he mused, "she could get to know you, if she was here all summer."

Molly squeezed his hand. "That, too," she said and found, to her surprise, that she meant it.

"I'm going to think about it," he promised.

They finished their coffee and discussed the Talia Wind case, exchanging ideas as to why Talia had left the library after midnight, when she obviously didn't intend to go home.

"She'd already done the medicine ceremony," Molly said, thinking aloud, "but for some reason she wasn't ready to leave yet." She suggested that Josh Rollins might have come to the library to talk to her and she'd walked back to his car with him. At which point, they'd argued and he'd killed her, or he'd left and somebody else had gotten there before Talia had returned to the library to get her bag.

"Or she saw or heard something outside as she was getting ready to go and went out to investigate," D.J. suggested.

"I don't know. After the attack at Eagle Rock and the notes, she'd be extremely leery of going outside if she thought there was somebody around—unless it was a person she trusted. Which brings us back to Josh Rollins."

"Could her going outside have had something to do with the medicine ceremony?"

It was a thought that hadn't occurred to Molly before. "I don't know. Her pipe and tobacco pouch were in the library basement. She probably performed the medicine ceremony there because that's where all the chair-scraping and chain-dragging sounds seemed to come from."

"I don't know anything about Cherokee medicine, but what if she finished the ceremony—released the ghost, or whatever—and then saw something that she thought was the ghost leaving the library. Would she have gone outside to make sure he was gone?"

Molly shook her head. "I just don't know, D.J. Talia was into a lot of New Age stuff, too. Maybe she did something else, something outside, in addition to the medicine ceremony."

D.J.'s words stayed with Molly and, later that night, after D.J. had left her apartment for work, she sat at her computer and brought up the Talia Wind file again. She scrolled to the last page and typed: *It was necessary for Talia to go outside to perform some final ceremony??? She saw or heard the ghost outside??? She went out to be sure the ghost left the premises???*

Molly stared at the questions she had typed. Had Talia actually seen or heard the ghost outside—or what she thought was the ghost? It was the one thing she would not have hesitated to leave the library for. She was there to communicate with the ghost, to release him or to learn what else must be done to effect his release. If she thought he was outside, she'd have gone out to face him.

Molly exited the file and turned off the computer.

In all the stories the library employees had told her about the ghost, there had been only one visible manifestation—the reflection Alice Mundy had seen in the glass door. But there had been many noises attributed to the ghost. Chairs scraping. Chains dragging.

Molly walked over to the couch, removed the cushions, and unfolded her bed, thinking all the while that she was missing something.

She heard Homer settling down on the landing outside her door as she got into bed. For a while, she gazed at the quarter-moon framed between two tree branches outside the window over the kitchen table and listened to the silence. But when she closed her eyes, she saw the Native American Research Library as she had seen it earlier that day from her car—as Natalie had seen it the previous night, until she fell asleep, and in leaving at dawn almost collided with a red Mercedes.

Behind Molly's closed eyelids, she saw the access road, the gate, the automobile showroom, the garages.

Her eyes flew open. The gate. She jumped out of bed, turned on the light, and dialed the Sheriff's Department.

A female dispatcher answered.

"This is Molly Bearpaw. Could I speak to Deputy Kennedy? We're working on a case together."

"I know about that. But he's not here right now. He and Brock went out on a stolen car call."

"Another one?"

"Yeah, a new Oldsmobile. The owner picked it up in Tulsa yesterday. Listen, I can page D.J. and ask him to call you when he gets time."

"No." Molly thought for a moment. "Tell him I'm going out to Dowell's to check on something. I'll talk to him later."

"You're going now? Do you know it's after midnight?"

"Just tell him, please."

"Okay, what's Dowell's?"

"D.J. will know what I mean."

Molly hung up, ran to her closet, and grabbed the first pair of jeans and shirt she saw. She was stuffing her car keys into a jeans pocket as she raced out of the apartment and almost fell over Homer.

"Oops, sorry, boy! You want to go for a ride?" Homer barked and flopped his tail. "Come on, then."

She clambered down the stairs, out to her car, opened the

door for Homer to jump into the passenger seat, went around to the other side, and started to drive.

The streets she traveled, going south out of town, were deserted, the businesses and houses dark. It was like a ghost town. She drove slowly, in no hurry. If she was right, she had all night to prove it to herself. Then she'd go to D.J. She didn't even think of waiting until she could talk to him. She could do this alone and she had to find out for herself—now—one way or the other. Time enough to tell D.J. if her wild wisp of an idea had any substance.

Reaching the highway, she continued south, past a few outlying businesses, a motel, a trading post, the Talking Leaves Job Corps Center, the Cherokee Nation's headquarters and gift shop.

She turned off on the road bordering the Native American Research Library and Dowell's, then made a sharp turn and backed into the narrow side road where she'd parked earlier that day, where Natalie had spent the previous night in her car. She pulled off on the shoulder, killed the motor, and turned off the lights.

Homer looked at her and whined quizzically. "It's okay, old buddy. We'll just look around a bit."

She pocketed her keys, had second thoughts and retrieved them to unlock the glove compartment. She stared at the Smith & Wesson for a long moment. She wouldn't need it, so why take it?

Don't ever pick up a gun unless you're prepared to use it. Her gun course instructor had said that repeatedly. Well, she wouldn't have to use it tonight, but she might someday, and she needed to get used to the feel of carrying it. She reached in and got the gun, checked the clip. Fully loaded, it held fourteen shells. At the moment, it contained nine. She snapped the clip back into place, found the butt pack she kept in her glove compartment with the gun and strapped it around her waist with the pocket in front. She secured the gun's safety, got out of the car, and tucked the gun into the pack's pocket, leaving the flap unsnapped. Then she stuffed her keys into a jeans pocket and pulled her shirt out and let it hang down to cover the pack.

"Come on, boy," she said to Homer. He jumped out of the car and stood beside her, waiting as she got his leash from the car and snapped it on his collar. Conrad had taught him to obey simple commands. "Heel," she said as she started walking, and he fell in close beside her on her left.

They crossed the intersecting road and walked along the access road between the library and the car dealership. As they drew near enough for Molly to see that the big gate was closed, relief poured through her. She halted and placed her hand lightly on Homer's head.

She'd been wrong after all.

As she stepped to one side and started to reverse her direction, she saw a light in a small, high-up window in one of the garages. It doesn't mean anything, she told herself. The mechanics just forgot to turn out the lights when they left. Tim said they do that a lot.

She walked up to the gate. The chain seemed to be hanging down on the right side of the gate which met the left side in the middle of the access road, but in the darkness she couldn't be sure. She ran her hand down between the metal posts where the two sides of the gates met. One side was slightly ajar. The chain had been moved and the padlock was hanging open, hooked on a link of the heavy chain.

She hesitated. Homer looked up at her and whined softly. "Shh," she cautioned him. She looped his leash around a gate post and said, "Stay, boy."

She pushed the gate open far enough to slip through. The chain dragged on the ground with the movement. The sound made her cringe. In the silence, it seemed loud enough to be heard a block away. Was that what Talia had heard Sunday night? She froze and waited, her eyes fixed on the dim front of the lighted garage. If someone was inside and he'd heard the gate being opened, he'd come out to investigate. But the door remained closed. She waited a few more minutes, thinking about Talia Wind.

She could imagine how it might have happened. Talia had performed the medicine ceremony, then heard the sound of chains dragging outside, and had come out to meet the ghost. Only it wasn't the ghost she'd heard. What happened then? Molly's imagination balked at that point, but whatever the sequence of events that night—if Molly's theory was true—it led to Talia's murder.

Homer sat outside the gate, peering up at her. "Stay," Molly whispered again. She moved off the gravel to walk quietly on the grass that edged the road. She crept around the paint shop, but there wasn't a window low enough for her to see inside.

Suddenly a noise from inside the paint shop made her heart leap in her chest. It sounded like something heavy, something made of metal, being dragged across a concrete floor. She thought she knew generally what was going on, but she wished she could see the man or men inside before she left to find D.J. Was it a mechanic? Or two or three of them? There were no cars parked nearby. They must have hidden them, in the alley probably.

Let it be the mechanics.

She hesitated. Now that she knew somebody was here, it was time to go for reinforcements. Reversing her direction, she circled around the building again. Just as she reached a front corner, the door ten feet to her left opened and, before she could move, a man stepped out in the spill of light. The smell of paint flowed out behind him.

"God Almighty!" he yelped. It was Kurt Cloud. His eyes flared, then narrowed as he stared at her. It was a frigid stare. "I *thought* I heard something."

Glancing past him into the shop, Molly gripped the corner of the building, her legs unsteady. "My—er, uh, my car broke down."

He grabbed her arm and pulled her into the light. "Well, if it ain't Molly Bearpaw." Molly's heart sank. She had hoped he wouldn't recognize her. He was still gripping her arm, and now he shoved her into the paint shop, followed her in, and pulled the door shut behind them.

Molly's eyes darted around the cavernous interior. In one corner, a big U-shaped contraption sat on runners. To her right was a white metal structure, about the size of a two-car garage. The big double doors to the garagelike structure were open, revealing a new, dark green Oldsmobile parked inside. Its windows were covered with brown paper, secured by masking tape. The wheels were covered, too, and masking tape covered all the chrome surfaces.

It had to be the car stolen earlier that night, and it was prepared for a new paint job. Kurt Cloud must have been

about to start the painting when he heard her and came outside to check.

Cloud, who was still behind her, nudged her toward the car
and the garagelike booth. "Now, what am I gonna do with
you?"

Her back to him, Molly stood between the open doors,
staring at the Oldsmobile. She slid her hand under the tail of
her shirt and touched the bulge of her gun. Carefully, she
moved her fingers under the pack flap and gripped the gun.
She turned around slowly, pulling out the gun as she did so.

"Get back," she said, struggling to control her voice. "I'm
leaving. I don't want to shoot you if I don't have to."

He stared at the gun, then lifted his cold eyes to hers. "I
don't think you're gonna shoot nobody." His voice was calm,
almost matter of fact. He took a tentative step toward her.
She released the safety catch with her thumb and, holding the
gun in both hands, she pointed it at his chest.

She heard her instructor's voice clearly. *Don't try to be a
sharpshooter. Go for the biggest target. Aim at the torso.*

"Get out of my way."

He hesitated, his eyes narrowing into slits. Then, with a
flickering glance over her shoulder and a sweep of one arm,
he stepped aside. Too late, Molly heard the rush of feet behind her, and, turning, saw the blur of the man who launched
himself at her. She went sprawling into the Oldsmobile,
bounced off and landed on her side beside a wheel. She'd lost
her grip on the gun and it slid under the Olds.

She tried to get up, rolled over on her back instead. The
pain around her hipbone, where she'd hit the car, was excru-
ciating. She groaned.

"Don't move." Tim Dowell's face swam somewhere above her.

She tried again to sit up. He planted a foot on her chest and pushed her back down.

"That's a stolen car," she said.

He shook his head. "I was starting to like you, Molly. But you just had to keep nosing around, didn't you?"

"Talia Wind heard you bringing in another car Sunday night and came over to investigate. Isn't that what happened? That was the night Dr. Ridley's Lincoln was stolen." Tim had left his father asleep in the house to come here. But Rayburn Dowell woke up, found Tim gone, and went out to look for him. The next time he and Cloud needed to paint a car, Tim had asked Helen Carmichael to spend the night, let her think he had a date.

Tim studied her for a long moment. "Think you've got it all figured out, don't you?"

"Convince me I'm wrong."

He shook his head sadly. "You should've learned a lesson from what happened to Talia Wind."

"I told you killing that conjuring woman was a mistake!" Kurt Cloud blurted.

"Shut up!" snarled Tim. His eyes darted around. He looked wild, scared, frantic. He looked like a stranger. He took his foot off Molly's chest and stepped back. "Quick! Close the doors!"

Molly grabbed the Olds's bumper and dragged herself to her feet. The doors slammed shut, imprisoning her in the metal booth. She heard the noise of something being pushed through the door handles, locking them closed.

"What're you gonna do?" Kurt Cloud asked.

"Dammit, Cloud, whatever I have to do," Tim said.

"I don't like this shit, Tim."

"Shut the hell up!"

Their voices faded.

Molly banged on one of the metal doors with her fists. "I left word with the Sheriff's Department that I was coming here!" she yelled.

"You're lying," Tim yelled. He had moved away from the doors.

Molly put her ear against metal and heard them moving around in the shop. What were they doing? How long would they leave her there? They were probably working out what to do with her, then they'd let her out.

She remembered the gun.

Tim had been so panicked, he'd forgotten about it. No, Molly didn't think he'd forget a thing like that. Okay, he meant to get it later. But why would he leave the gun inside with Molly? Because she couldn't shoot him if she couldn't see him.

And he didn't mean for her to leave that booth alive. Once they decided to come in, they'd rush her before she could get off a shot.

She dropped to her knees, and then lay down on her stomach, gritting her teeth against the pain as she inched her way under the Olds, right arm extended. She gripped the gun butt, and lay there for a moment, gasping and letting the pain subside to a tolerable level. Then, gritting her teeth again, she squirmed out from under the car. She got to her feet and leaned against a fender. Resting her arms on the hood of the Olds, she aimed the gun at the doors and waited for them to open. She couldn't see any way they could kill her while she was inside and they were outside the booth. They had to open those doors sometime.

She waited . . . and waited . . .

She saw now that her prison had a roof, and there were exhaust fans on either end to disperse the fumes after a paint job.

She heard a shuffling noise and her gaze shot back to the door.

Next came a whooshing sound and a sudden, strong stink. Like paint thinner. She stared at the door, but it didn't open. The whooshing sound didn't stop, and the stink was getting worse. It was coming from outside, through the narrow crack between the doors. They didn't plan to rush her at all. They didn't plan to open those doors until she was dead.

Oh, God! They'd rigged up a way to pump her prison full of toxic fumes. Every breath brought her closer to death.

Coughing, she pressed the tail of her cotton shirt over her mouth and stumbled toward one side of the booth. Even with the cloth over her mouth, the stink was almost unbearable.

She searched frantically for a way to activate the exhaust fans, but no switch was visible. The fans must be operated from outside. Panic raced through Molly. She would be unconscious within minutes.

Stay calm, she told herself. Think!

She hunched over to see if the fumes were weaker near the floor, but it didn't seem to make much difference. Her shirt clung to her, damp from perspiration, and it was getting harder to breathe. She was getting dizzy, too. Soon she would pass out, and then she would die.

All right, she told herself, you are going to die. But not without doing everything you can think of to save yourself.

Think. Think. It was difficult. A fog seemed to have invaded her brain, and her throat felt swollen, and every breath burned like fire.

Think, Molly.

She had her gun and—what was it now?—nine shells. Shooting wild through the walls of the booth was no good. They wouldn't be where she could hit them.

Think, Molly. But what she really wanted to do was lie down, let go.

Think!

Every indrawn, fiery breath was expelled on a racking, gagging cough and water streamed from her burning eyes.

She steadied herself on the Olds and squinted at the narrow crack through which the lethal liquid was being pumped into the booth. She could see the source of the fumes now, a fine mist pouring into the booth through the crack about a foot above the floor. The container was sitting on the floor, the nozzle pressed up to the crack. Maybe she could push her finger through the crack and knock the container over.

Dizzy, staggering, she clamped the tail of her shirt over her mouth and made it to the door. Paint thinner drenched her legs, all the way up to her waist. Eyes squeezed shut, her breath trapped in her chest, she jammed the gun into her waistband and bent over. She stuck the tip of her finger into the crack. Paint thinner wet the front and arms of her shirt.

The crack wasn't as wide as it had looked; she could insert only the tip of her finger. Not enough to move the nozzle. And she'd held her breath as long as she could.

A sob tore through her. She straightened, exhaled a rush of

air and began to gag. Her legs wobbled, too weak now to hold her upright. She fell against the door. She moved her head to bring one slitted eye to the crack, above the spraying nozzle. She could see nothing but the wall of the shop and whatever they had grabbed to thread through the door handles to keep her locked in. It was round, about three inches thick. The handle of a mop or a broom.

Her head swam. Her thoughts were sluggish, drifting toward unconsciousness.

It took a moment for it to register.

Wood. The handle jammed through the door handles was wood.

Molly brought the gun up in both shaking hands. She pressed the barrel to the crack and the wood handle. She squeezed the trigger and kept squeezing, setting off explosion after explosion, until nothing sounded but a dull click when she squeezed.

Summoning her final scrap of strength, she rammed her shoulder against the crack. The doors gave and she fell, sprawling on the concrete floor. The container of paint thinner rolled away from her. She didn't see the men. They must have gone outside to wait for her to die.

With a sob, she got to her feet and stumbled toward the shop door. She still had the empty gun in her hand. Her finger was frozen, curled round the trigger.

She kicked at the outer door until it opened. She reeled through the opening into the blessed night air.

She stood, swaying, gulping it in.

She heard a man's curse and Kurt Cloud came running, lunged for her, his face a twisted mask. She threw her gun at his face. Blood gushed from his nose. He cursed and staggered back, his hands grabbing his face.

Homer, still tied to the gate post, barked frantically.

Molly gulped more air, drawing it deep into her sore lungs. As she stumbled backward, she heard running footsteps. She pulled the key ring from her jeans pocket and when Tim Dowell rounded the corner of the shop, she sprayed him with pepper gas. He screamed, cursed, but kept coming blindly.

Somehow she evaded his grasping hands and wobbled in the direction of the gate. Her legs felt like rubber.

Then Kurt Cloud seemed to come out of nowhere again, his face covered with blood. He planted himself between her and the gate.

She stopped. She wasn't going to make it.

But she had to keep trying. She wouldn't let them see she'd given up. If she could get to the fence, maybe she could climb over.

As she turned to run the other way, a yell of rage split the night and D.J. charged through the gate, with Homer barking furiously at his heels.

Homer leaped at Kurt, his teeth snapping, and brought him down.

It seemed to happen in slow motion. D.J., gun drawn, barking commands. Tim Dowell and Kurt Cloud lying facedown on the concrete, D.J. handcuffing them.

Then he turned to Molly. "My God, you're soaked. What is that smell?"

"Paint thinner." Her teeth chattered.

"Are you all right?"

She nodded. "I will be," she said. "They killed Talia Wind.

She caught them painting a stolen car." She had begun to shake uncontrollably, and she started to cry.

He put his arm around her. "Shh, sweetheart. It's all right now."

*You have put the Intruder into a crevice in a high mountain
that it may never find the way back.
You have put it to rest in the Darkening Land, never to return.
Let the relief come.*

19

Molly went to the office Sunday morning to write her report on the Talia Wind case. Natalie dashed in a few minutes later. Molly had phoned the Winds in Idabel Friday night to let them know Talia's murderers had been arrested.

"I didn't think you'd be back in town till Monday," Molly said.

"I had to come back early to study. I picked up a paper on the way through town." She thrust the City/State section of the Tulsa paper in front of Molly. "Have you seen this?"

"No." Molly picked up the paper and saw her picture, the one taken by the photographer for the local newspaper, along with an article about her ordeal and the part she'd played in the arrest of Tim Dowell and Kurt Cloud. The Sheriff was quoted as saying, "We're always glad to cooperate with the Cherokee Nation," which made Molly smile. The headline said, "Murder and Mayhem in Cherokee County." The byline carried the name of a Tahlequah reporter, a stringer for the *Tulsa World*, who'd interviewed her yesterday.

She looked up at Natalie, who smiled and said, "You're famous."

"For ten minutes, fifteen tops."

"They even mentioned me in the last paragraph," Natalie said. "Well, not by name, but you're quoted as saying your assistant gave you a crucial clue that helped you solve the case. Did you really say that?"

"Sure did. That Mercedes that almost ran you down got me to thinking about the Mercedes that was stolen."

"So that's why you asked me if the car I saw was blue?"

Molly nodded. "But you said *your* Mercedes was red. I can't remember the last time I saw a new Mercedes in Tahlequah, and within days two were seen. It bugged me. Then I remembered that paint shop at Dowell's and thought, maybe it was the same car—the blue car was now red. That's what set me on the right track."

Natalie grinned. "Cool. So, do I get a raise?"

Molly laughed. "Take it up with the council." Molly pointed at the door. "After you get your cramming done and pass all your courses. As for me, soon as I finish this report, I'm going back to bed."

"I didn't want to say anything, but you do look kind of the worse for wear."

"You try breathing paint thinner till you almost pass out, see how you feel."

Natalie headed for the door. "I'll take your word for it."

She opened the door, adding over her shoulder, "Just think. I can spend twenty-five hours every week all summer long, helping you with your investigations."

Molly looked at the closed door. "Can't wait," she muttered.

Three days later, Molly sat in a booth at The Shack with D.J. and her father. Dinner was her father's treat.

It had taken the full week and at least a dozen showers before Molly stopped thinking she could smell paint thinner.

Since her father was paying for dinner, she'd ordered a bowl of chicken noodle soup and coffee, insisting that she wasn't very hungry. D.J. and her father had ordered burgers and fries.

When her father had called yesterday to invite her to dinner, he'd questioned her about what had happened at Dowell's. She'd replied with as few words as possible and he'd let it go.

Now, while D.J. and her father finished the cherry pie they'd ordered for dessert, Molly, holding her coffee cup in both hands, finally talked about that night.

At length her father said, "So, you thought you'd see if anybody was there and then you meant to leave and call the Sheriff's Department."

"Yes. I kept hoping it would be the mechanics, but that was just wishful thinking. It didn't enter my mind that Kurt Cloud was in on it. Somebody with keys to all the buildings and the authority to use them at night had to be involved, and that meant Tim Dowell or his employees. And whoever killed Talia had lured her outside somehow. I couldn't believe she'd trusted anybody except Josh Rollins enough to go out. But it finally occurred to me that if Josh had wanted to kill her, he could have done it at the restaurant and driven out of town somewhere to dispose of the body. Once I'd virtually eliminated Rollins and the other suspects in my mind, that left what D.J. had suggested. The ghost—or somebody Talia thought was the ghost—was responsible for her going outside with nothing but her flashlight."

"I still don't understand how that led you to suspect somebody at Dowell's," D.J. put in.

"It was the chain on the gate to the access road," Molly said. "I'd noticed it earlier that day when I drove out to look around. I wasn't looking for anything in particular, and I didn't connect it with Talia right away." She glanced at D.J., who sat beside her. "It wasn't until after we returned from Claremore and you went to work that I remembered the library employees had reported hearing what sounded like chains dragging when they were working alone in the library at night. Once I remembered that, I put it together with the chain on that gate. That's what Talia heard Sunday night. She thought it was the ghost, and that's why she went outside. But I still wasn't sure of it at that point. I really couldn't believe Tim Dowell would be involved in criminal activity. He told me his business was doing well, so why would he risk losing it?"

"He lied about his business. Since his arrest, we've learned that he's nearly bankrupt," D.J. said. "I guess he figured he'd get back on his feet by stealing cars for a while. But he needed a partner, somebody to steal the cars and bring them to the paint shop."

"Kurt Cloud," Molly said. "He took an auto mechanics course in prison."

Rob frowned. "Why didn't you talk to D.J. before you went out there?"

"I tried," Molly said, bridling a little at his parental tone. He'd lost the right to criticize her, if that's what he was doing. "I called the Sheriff's Department and the dispatcher said he was out checking on a report that a new Oldsmobile had been stolen. That's when I realized that, if I was right, that Oldsmobile was probably in the paint shop at Dowell's at that very moment."

"How did you know they were painting the cars?" her father asked. "Instead of just tearing them down to sell the parts?"

"It was something Natalie Wind said. She's my assistant and Talia Wind's niece," she added for her father's benefit. "She spent Wednesday night parked on that side road near the library with some crazy notion that the murderer might return to the scene of the crime. She was right, but she didn't know it because she fell asleep. If she hadn't, she would probably have seen the Mercedes that was stolen that night being driven into the paint shop. She did see it the next morning as she was leaving. The driver almost sideswiped her as she pulled out of the side road."

"Kurt Cloud," D.J. put in. "He drove the cars to their connection in Kansas City after they were painted. Their cohort got forged titles and sold the cars there, kept a third and split the rest with Dowell and Cloud. Cloud told us that much when we questioned him after his arrest. He also said that it was Dowell who killed Talia. Then his attorney showed up and he hasn't said another word. Dowell has kept his lip zipped from the beginning."

"Kurt Cloud would lie to save his own skin," Molly said,

"but I think he's telling the truth about Tim being the one who killed Talia. Cloud mentioned it Thursday night, when they were trying to decide what to do with me."

D.J. nodded. "I figure the DA will work out a deal with Cloud's attorney. Cloud's testimony against Dowell in the murder for a reduced charge on the car thefts."

"Tell me something, Molly," Rob said. "How'd you know the car that almost hit Natalie was stolen?"

"I didn't for sure. But I knew that a new blue Mercedes had been stolen that night and when Natalie mentioned a Mercedes, I asked her if it was blue. She said no, it was red. I tried to dismiss it at first. But I kept coming back to that Mercedes. How many new Mercedes are there in Tahlequah? In Cherokee County, for that matter. I already knew Dowell's had a paint shop—I noticed the sign when I was out there earlier. Once I started thinking that Talia must have gone outside because she heard chains dragging, and put that together with the chain on Dowell's gate, I started asking myself why somebody would have been using that gate at night—and what Talia could have seen or heard that got her killed. It almost had to be something illegal. So I called D.J. and the dispatcher said another car had been stolen."

D.J. gave her a look. "And you couldn't wait for me to get back before you dashed out there?"

"I thought I couldn't—at the time. And I only wanted to see if I could find the car before I talked to you."

"You almost got yourself killed," Rob said.

"Yeah, well that's one of the risks you take in my line of work." It came out sharper than she'd intended. She added, "I had Homer and my gun. I felt safe."

"Unfortunately, you tied Homer to the gate and he couldn't

get loose," D.J. said. "When I got there, he was trying to chew his leash in two. Thank God, you took the gun."

"I never thought I'd be happy I carried a gun," Molly said and explained for her father how she'd shot her way out of the paint booth. She smiled at D.J. "That gun saved my life, along with Deputy Kennedy here and Homer."

"Listen, Molly," her father said. "You were lucky this time. But you ought to be more careful in the future."

Molly gazed across the table at her father. His dark eyes were deeply concerned, and the curt retort she was tempted to make died before it was spoken.

In the last week, more old memories of her father had surfaced, and they were good memories. Even though he had left, even though he'd been too weak to stay and be a father, he had loved her, she knew that. And the face across the table from her—the face that was twenty-five years older than the one in her memories—belonged to a man who wanted to make his peace.

Give the guy a break, D.J. kept saying. And she had made up her mind to do that. Which meant she had to put recriminations behind her somehow. She might think them for a long while yet, but she didn't have to say them.

"I will," she said. "And I'm going to go to the firing range more often, too. I thought I would never be able to shoot a human being." She shook her head. "But last Thursday night, I could have done it without a second thought if I'd had the chance."

She shivered and D.J. put his arm around her.

Watching them, Robert Bearpaw smiled.

"Natalie told me today that Ridge spent last night in the library. He wanted to see if the ghost was gone," Molly said.

"What happened?" D.J. asked.

"Nothing. No chairs scraping, no reflections in glass. Ridge said he got a peaceful feeling from being there, something he'd never felt before. Ridge is convinced that Talia released the ghost before she was killed." Molly was no longer sure he was wrong.

D.J.'s mouth curved up on one corner. He was reserving judgment.

"You haven't smoked a cigarette all evening," Molly said to her father.

"Put 'em down when I walked in that jail cell and haven't picked 'em up since. It's hard sometimes, but I keep those cinnamon discs to suck on and that helps."

"I'm glad *something* good came out of your time in jail," Molly said.

"Yeah," Rob agreed. He gazed at Molly. "You look tired, Miss Molly." He glanced at D.J. "She could use some shut-eye. I think you better take her home."

They left the café. Molly and D.J. said goodbye to Rob on the street. The apartment he had rented was half a block away, just around the corner from Muskogee Avenue.

D.J. had the night off. But on her landing, he said, "Your dad's right. I'm going home and let you get some rest." He kissed her, waited for her to unlock her door, then ran down the stairs to his car.

A few minutes later, she went out to make sure Homer had plenty of water for the night. She petted him and talked to him for a few minutes, but didn't let him come inside.

Alone again in her apartment, she lay down on the couch with a throw pillow for her head. She'd pull the bed out later. She closed her eyes and thought about tomorrow, and next week, next year. Everything would be different now that her father was back.

She was glad she hadn't said those mean words tonight. Maybe, in time, she wouldn't even think them. She might even like Rob Bearpaw once she came to know him better. Maybe they would become good friends.

Rob Bearpaw, she thought then, her father.

What was the happiest thing that happened to you today, Miss Molly?

A smile tugged at the corners of her mouth. He'd made the first move with dinner tonight. Now it was her turn. She would cook dinner for him one day soon. She didn't like to cook, so it would be something simple. She didn't think that would matter to him at all.

Robert Bearpaw. *Dad.* Would she ever be able to call him that to his face.

Maybe. Someday.